THE DSA SEASON TWO, BOOK FOUR

C R A C K E D

# CHRYSALIS

# Also by Lou Paduano

## The Greystone Saga

*Signs of Portents*
*Tales from Portents*
*The Medusa Coin*
*Pathways in the Dark*
*A Circle of Shadows*

## Greystone-in-Training

*Hammer and Anvil*
*The Gifts of Kali*
*The Final Gauntlet*

## The DSA

**Season One**
*The Clearing*
*Promethean*
*The Bridge*
*Spectral Advocate*
*Dark Impulses*
*Broken Loyalties*

**Season Two**
*The Wellspring*
*Foundations*
*The Missing*

THE DSA SEASON TWO, BOOK FOUR

# CRACKED CHRYSALIS

Lou Paduano

Eleven Ten Publishing LLC

GRAND ISLAND, NEW YORK

Eleven Ten Publishing LLC
282 Fareway Lane
Grand Island, NY 14072

Publisher's note: This is a work of fiction. Names, characters, places, and incidents either are the product of the author's imagination or are used fictitiously. Any resemblance to actual events, locales, or persons, living or dead, is entirely coincidental.

Printed in the United States of America
Cover art design by MiblArt

First edition published 2024

Library of Congress Cataloguing in Publication Data
Paduano, Lou
Cracked Chrysalis / Lou Paduano

LCCN: 2024907019
ISBN-13: 978-1-944965-43-3 (paperback)
ISBN-13: 978-1-944965-42-6 (eBook)

*For Louise*

# CHAPTER ONE

The walls closed in on Ben Riley. He felt the pressure build all around him, from the confining corridors to the constant hum of the air filtration units that kept the team from suffocating. Everywhere Ben looked, there was no escape. He meandered through the space, lost to everything that had happened recently and the hopelessness he had been left with in the aftermath.

Emily Wright was still missing. His time in Kansas with Morgan had proved to be wasted. The purpose of their visit brought no closure for Ben. He pined for answers and some sign of life from his former partner, yet without another lead, Ben could do nothing but worry.

Emily was merely the tip of the iceberg, though. Since Ben's brush with death, there was also the Trust to deal with. The mysterious organization had stolen his life away. Ben believed the DSA to be his second chance to make things right. Little evidence corroborated that sentiment. Following his recruitment, he had been beaten, shot, and forced to hide from the world.

The sting of defeat infected every aspect of his life like a cancer in his soul. The Bunker offered nothing to quell the anger swelling inside him. Hiding solved nothing in Ben's eyes. Every quiet moment offered only additional anxiety that caused his fists to clench and his pacing to loop through the complex repeatedly.

He tried to work through it. Training had never been one of his strong suits and it showed in the workout room of the massive underground complex. The lifelike robotics firmly kicked the living crap out of him. Fighting solved nothing and left Ben with only fresh bruises and overwhelming frustration.

Answers were what he required. Some lead on the Trust, or Emily, or every other threat that circled them, would put his mind to work on a problem instead of spinning his wheels with nothing concrete to do.

Ben left the workout room defeated and depressed, and started toward the Operations Hub. There, he found Alison Adler at her terminal. With the time she spent in front of the monitors, she most likely slept there as well. All served her own fruitless mission—some mystery signal that no one seemed able to track.

She picked at a bag of trail mix, wiping the crumbs along her jeans. Her clean hand typed away at the keyboard for her answers. She wasn't alone in the expansive chamber.

Across the way, steam rose in the kitchen. A pan sizzled, constantly moved by Robert Kanigher. He was working on his latest creation, another pain-staking meal to keep his thoughts focused and his body moving. Ben hated the ease at which Kanigher relaxed during their downtime. What he hated more was the incredible smell emanating from the pan. It certainly surpassed the Hot Pocket Ben had found deep in the freezer unit for his meal.

Ben waited impatiently in the center of the room. Neither member of the team threw him a single glance. They were caught up in their own worlds, working on their own projects, while he did nothing constructive on any level. His frustration, and knowing it to be only his own, caused Ben to throw up his hands.

"That's it!" he yelled. "I've had it. I'm done."

Kanigher sighed. He lowered the heat on the stove and let the pan settle. "Here we go again."

Ben's gaze thinned. "Stuff it, Chef Boy-R-Dee. This bunker is giving me claustrophobia."

"You should have left with Morgan," Kanigher grumbled.

"She didn't tell me she was leaving," Ben said. He moved for the counter. His hands grabbed the edge, his eyes on the steaks in the pan and not on Kanigher.

It had been a lie. Morgan had reached out to him for a day trip to the city. Ben's reaction at hearing the destination had been a firm rejection. Morgan's concern about Ben's health continued, and another trip to a doctor's office had been the last thing Ben wanted to deal with after everything. Putting his near-death experience behind him was more to his liking, along with every dark thought the close call propagated.

Ben shook his head. "Her little trip is beside the point, anyway."

"How so?" Kanigher asked, the words lacking any emotion.

"When the DSA went kablooey, no one, I repeat no one, said that was the end of our normal lives. Yet here we are, cut off, passing the time between missions instead of living."

"Get a hobby."

"Like cooking? Pass," Ben said with a laugh. He leaned over the stove and pointed to the meal. "I'd like mine well done, by the way."

"Not a chance," Kanigher shot back. "Sucks the flavor right out."

"That's what barbecue sauce is for."

Kanigher pulled the pan away. His cold eyes stared through Ben for a long moment. Slowly Ben's words sank in, and when they did, Kanigher shook his head. "I can't talk to you right now."

The practicing chef turned his back on the room. Ben stood, waiting for another biting comment. Kanigher remained silent, however.

Ben backed away from the counter for Operations. "Great. That leaves me with Adler."

"Huh?" she called without looking.

"Still searching for your mysterious signal?" A nod escaped her, again clearly not caring to look away from her monitors. "What a life."

Ben tapped along the metal railing. He whistled a tune, nothing from his collection of music, but a little riff to fill the silence of the space and overshadow the clacking of the keyboard.

Adler's hands fell away from the keys. She pushed away from the station. Her chair bumped into the conference table. Fixing her position, Adler lifted her legs to the side of the table.

"I actually don't mind this, Ben," she said with the innocent smile she always carried. He never understood Adler's desire to join their team. She was too young, and too nice, in a world that displayed nothing but contempt for those qualities. "Being down here has really focused me on what is important."

"Like terminal eye strain from staring at computer screens all day long?"

Adler laughed. "I could get that anywhere in the country. No, I'm talking about the kinds of things we never found the time to do in life. Like all those books you always say you're going to read, but never found the time because of grocery shopping, working all day, the gym at night, pets, relationships, all that stuff."

Adler jumped to her feet. She shifted in front of Ben. Her eyes caught his and held tight. Ben tried to pull away, to go back to the disinterest of Kanigher, but it was too late. He was in it for the long haul, caught in the enthusiasm of Adler.

"Do you know what I just finished?"

"I get the feeling you'll tell me," Ben mumbled.

"Carl Sagan's *Cosmos*," Adler exclaimed. She waited for a reaction. Ben offered nothing in response. "You know the one. About his theories in explaining God through our physical surroundings. Talk about mind-blowing. The book changed my entire outlook on universal mechanics. You know?"

Ben's blank stare eventually penetrated her unmatched joy. Her smile faded, and she fell back a step.

"Never mind."

"No," Ben said. He started down the steps. "I get it, Adler. I just finished this amazing book as well."

Adler cocked an eyebrow. "Really?"

"I did," Ben balked. "There was some heady talk about the universe as well. Well, at least from one of the four main characters. The rest were all about saving the universe from all manner of threats. Parts were pretty political too. There's this Eastern European dictator always trying to destroy them."

"Ben..."

"Absolutely fascinating stuff," Ben continued. "You can borrow it if you'd like. I think it would be right up your alley."

Adler crossed her arms. "Ben, you're talking about the *Fantastic Four*."

Ben smiled. "Doesn't make it any less important."

"I never—"

The outer door opened and ended their discussion. All turned at the sound, the unexpected arrival caught in the frame. He carried a laptop bag over his shoulder. His eyes drooped from a lack of sleep, but he continued to needle a tablet as he walked. It was the only way Nixon Jessup traveled.

He didn't bother to wave a greeting to them. Nixon made no eye contact with anyone in the room, while he barreled deeper into the complex.

"Nixon?" Adler asked with concern.

Ben cut off the newcomer. "Welcome back, Nixon. You can settle a debate we're having on the Marvel Age of Comics."

"I..."

Kanigher left the comfort of the kitchen. "What happened on the mission, Nixon? Is Susan all right?"

Nixon lowered his work and rubbed his neck. "Yeah. She's... she's fine. Coming down now."

"Good," Ben said. He wrapped an arm around the man and pulled him close. "I wanted to talk to you about the workout room. Those bots of yours could be put to better use than beating the hell out of us, couldn't they? I'm talking full-on interactive scenarios. Like that space show. You know the one I'm talking about."

"*Star Trek?*" Adler said, exasperation in her voice. "You're lecturing me over *Fantastic Four* and you don't know *Star Trek?*"

"I knew you did," Ben said with a wink.

"Guys, listen..." Nixon started. He shifted away from Ben, his gaze still low to the ground. "Something happened during the mission that—"

"Well, I doubt it compares to what's been going on in this always interesting bunker of ours," Ben said.

Adler sighed. "It's been a day, Nixon."

"I couldn't have put it better myself, young lady," a voice called from the door. Attention returned to the entrance. The man filling the frame lifted his fedora from his head. The Witness' opaque glasses reflected the overhead lights of the Bunker. "Hello."

Ben started for the man. "Kanigher?"

"On it." Kanigher reached into his apron. He pulled out a Glock and tossed it over to Ben. Then he grabbed a second pistol from beneath the counter.

Ben caught the Glock in mid-stride and took aim. A glance around the room told him Kanigher and Adler had joined him in covering the intruder in their midst.

"Oh, it is so clobberin' time," Ben said. The weapon was inches from the Witness' forehead, yet the man didn't flinch at the threat. He made no move to withdraw or confront the agent.

"Don't you dare, Riley," Susan Metcalf barked from behind the pair. Bare feet stamped across the tile. The tight red dress she wore was torn along the slip, showing off her legs to the crowd. She circled the Witness, then shuffled the man back to split them up. "He's here as my guest."

"Susan?" Kanigher called from the kitchen. "What are you —"

"If this is about the dress, table it," Metcalf replied sharply. Kanigher's eyes continue to bulge at the sight of the open back of her outfit.

Containing a comment or three for his shocked colleague, Ben focused on the enemy in their midst. He kept the gun on the Witness, his finger tight to the trigger.

"Put it down, Ben."

His jaw clenched in anger. "Are you kidding me? We're having a sleepover party with this guy?"

"Susan," Kanigher said. "Is this on the level?"

"It is, Bobby," she replied. "Please."

They lowered their weapons. Kanigher acted first; Metcalf's word was enough for him. Adler followed suit, the weapon shaky under her grasp from the onset. Ben, however, held tight to his sidearm and his mounting rage.

The Witness had committed atrocities that had taken the lives of thousands. Yet, he had also saved Ben's life. Ben was more than happy to resolve the conflict brought up by the two events given the opportunity.

Metcalf, though, refused to let that scenario play out. She helped Ben lower the gun. Her eyes never left him, cold blue steel that never wavered and never showed weakness no matter the situation.

"Ben," she said in a calming voice. "He needs our help."

# CHAPTER TWO

The van screeched to a halt. Hurried steps carried Morgan from the vehicle to the front door of the Wilmut Clinic. Urgency brought her back, and an unwillingness to let anything else distract her from the task.

Tests had been run on Ben's blood. They were necessary. Her fear of the side-effects from the Witness' miracle drug was too great to ignore. She'd pushed and prodded until, finally, her partner agreed. The tests, however, took time and a promise had been made to return for the results after a week.

Almost two had passed in the interim. Their time in Wichita might have saved the life of a young college student, but it had distracted Morgan from her concerns over Ben.

Still, her worries rested on the unknown quantity of the drug in Ben's system. She couldn't take the chance that he was a walking time-bomb, couldn't pretend there might not be a risk to others as well. Too many variables cropped up when it came to the Witness. She'd almost lost Ben once and refused to allow it to happen again.

She had called ahead of her arrival, which helped clear her way through the reception area. Her badge answered all remaining questions. The pair of personnel behind the counter offered no resistance, their questions silenced with the sight of the FBI insignia — false though it may have been.

She recalled the layout of the center. Morgan had escorted an elderly patient to the place recently. Wesley Fuller had turned out to be more than that in the end, one of the first agents of the DSA with casework dating back to the 1970s. He had also been a man in need, and someone Morgan had been glad to assist.

The rush in her gait slowed. Narrow corridors forced her to hug tight to the wall. A constant flow of patients and doctors threw her looks of agitation and confusion, but again, none moved to stop her.

Shouting turned out to be the only thing that halted her forward momentum. The raised voices filled the back half of the center. Heads poked out from closed offices, curious stares at the heated argument from the lab that consumed the rear space.

"What the hell is this, Simon?" Morgan heard a woman shout.

Morgan rounded the corner for the lab, stopped in the doorway, then shifted back to the hall. She stuck close to the opening but remained out of view.

She recognized the man at the center of the argument: Simon Holbrook. He was a lanky fellow, nervous and twitching in his movements. Sweat dotted his brow and filled his palms. Morgan had only met the short, stubby woman next to him briefly, but recalled her to be less than congenial to guests in the clinic.

"It's not what you think," Simon said. He pulled the sample set away from her and tucked it behind his back. "I—"

"No," the woman snapped. "I don't want to hear it, Simon."

"Anne—"

"Those were unmarked samples," Anne said with a shake of her head. While Simon's eyes pleaded with her, his superior didn't bother to look at him. Her words drove her point home. "You've been running tests without approval. Nothing to the insurance company. Nothing from me. Are you experimenting again?"

"No, I wouldn't do that," Simon said. He dropped the samples along the counter. When he returned to Anne, his hands were open wide like his eyes. "I would never—"

"I thought you understood, Simon," Anne replied, not caring for an explanation. "After what happened last time, I thought you understood the consequences of your actions."

"I do," Simon said. "I do understand. That's not what this is."

Anne pushed through him. Leaning along the counter, she searched through the contents of the desk. "I came in here for a reason. Where are the samples for Mrs. Conover?"

The name spurred Simon to hurry. He shifted a pile of reports aside until he found the one requested. Simon passed it along without a word.

The grouchy superior pawed through the documents. "What did you do?"

"My job," Simon said. "You thought—"

"It was a simple case of IBS," Anne said.

"It wasn't IBS." He pointed to the front page of his analysis. "Mrs. Conover has Celiac Disease."

Anne choked back her anger for a moment, aghast. "That's not... Simon, you're not authorized to make—"

Simon shook his head. "It's easily mistaken for Irritable Bowel Syndrome. I thought it warranted a closer look and ran an extra test. I can recheck the sample if you're unsure about my findings."

Anne threw the report at his desk. "This is unacceptable. Simon, your work is... well, it's amazing. Unfortunately, you've turned into a liability that I can no longer afford."

"Anne?" Simon's voice cracked. "Wait. Don't do this, Anne."

"No choice."

"Yes, there is. You can—"

Anne started for the door without another glance back. "Security will be here in five minutes. Pack up your stuff."

Morgan ducked around the corner. The last thing she wanted was to raise the ire of the woman, so she kept out of sight as the stout woman stomped down the corridor to her office. Anne's phone was in hand, security's notification already in place by the time the door shut behind her.

A soft curse escaped Morgan's lips. She knew immediately who the unmarked samples belonged to, and why Simon had maintained their secrecy. Morgan quietly made her way back to the lab.

"Simon, I..."

The medical technician caught sight of her in the door, and his gaze fell to the floor. "You heard all that? Hell, everyone did, didn't they?"

"I'm so sorry," Morgan said. She shifted by his side and her hand fell on his shoulder. "I never meant for this to happen."

Simon pulled away at her touch. He collected an empty box from the corner of the room and placed the remnants of Ben's blood sample inside. Then he retrieved the analysis and tossed it at her. "Here."

Morgan caught the findings. "Is this—"

"The real reason you came."

The words stung, but the report overcame her concerns. She flipped through the thorough examination of Ben's blood. A quick scan only brought more questions. "Were there any abnormalities? Any signs of, well, anything?"

"It was clean," Simon said. He didn't bother looking at her. He quickly emptied drawers, dropping files into the box on top of the crimson-filled test tubes.

"Clean?" *Impossible.* Ben should have died from his injuries. Ignoring Simon for a moment, Morgan continued to search through the analysis. Everything lined up. There was nothing out of the ordinary. The miracle drug appeared to be safe, and so did Ben. The corner of Morgan's lips curled. "I can't thank you enough for this, Simon. I—"

Two shadows loomed in the doorway. Their radios chirped at their sides, but they ignored the summons. The pair of security guards already had their task set before them.

"Doctor Holbrook?" one asked. "It's time."

Simon nodded. He lifted the lone box of belongings, the entirety of his time at the clinic. "Don't thank me, Agent Dunleavy. Just don't."

Morgan watched the man as he left, escorted from the building like a criminal. All thanks to her. That image of Simon—another innocent victim of the DSA—stuck with Morgan for the rest of the day.

# CHAPTER THREE

The entire trip had been one of silent aggravation. No explanations had been made, not from Metcalf and especially not from their so-called guest. Instead, all that had been mentioned was a place called Millington, and the importance of moving as quickly as possible to intercede on the Witness' behalf.

Ben had held back his responses. There had been more than words to share with both sides of the coin, yet he remained silent for the time being. Part of Ben had hoped someone else would step up to remind the team who they were fighting for and against. No one had. No one had come to the rescue to bring them back to their sanity.

Nixon and Adler had worked to make the arrangements. They handled everything from the flights to the twin rental vans that came to a grinding halt in the vacant parking lot in front of a lumber mill just north of the town in Tennessee. Loading bays were empty; their metal doors slammed and locked shut.

Morgan and Ben led the way to the front. Morgan checked the lock on the door. It held firm, so she backed away and gave her partner a nod. Ben led with his foot, crashing just above the handle. When it failed to give, he leaped shoulder-first. The door finally collapsed, and the pair of agents split to cover the rest of the team.

The Witness stepped forward. He stared at the shattered door. A small object dangled from his fingertips. "I have the key."

Metcalf ushered him into the facility. At her merest touch, the man fell silent. Ben was grateful for the small favor.

"Sweep the perimeter," Metcalf said.

Kanigher offered a nod of approval. "I'll take left. You two…"

"Right," Ben confirmed. "Got it."

The tension level kept everyone on edge. Every response held back more than enough frustration to fill the room—even with a space as large as the lumber mill.

Machines occupied the room, from miters to the larger saws which dealt with the trunks. Refining the product seemed to take up much of the back half. Sawdust covered the ground, but there was no actual lumber present.

The Witness moved to follow the sweeping agents. Metcalf barred his approach. "Stay here until we lock it down."

The man with the opaque lenses smiled, then freed himself from her grasp. Fixing his cuff, the Witness headed down the center of the staging room.

Metcalf sighed. "Or just go where you want."

Ben caught Morgan's stare at the exchange. It was the same as had been on display throughout their travels. With every suggestion made by Metcalf, the Witness followed his own course. He never agreed to anything and refused to bend or compromise regardless of his so-called need for assistance.

As the Witness wandered the floor, Morgan glanced back to Ben. "What the hell are we doing here?"

He had been waiting for the question. Not only today, but for weeks it had been weighing on him. The Witness had saved Ben's life. *Why? What had inspired the man's change of heart?* With their past, they should have remained eternal enemies. That had been the vow Ben had made in the wake of the seven thousand lives lost in Bellbrook. Somehow, though, the Witness had walked away with something different from their meeting. He'd seen Ben's potential. He'd saved him to see that potential realized, but for whose purpose remained unknown.

"I wish I knew," was the best Ben could offer Morgan.

"Seriously? Why have we not put this guy on ice? He killed a town."

There had been more to it than that for Morgan. There had also been the man's connection with Lincoln—the true reason Morgan reviled the Witness. If Lincoln had come in, if he had believed in the DSA enough, he might have still been alive. Morgan clearly hadn't worked through those feelings, and they centered on one person in particular.

Morgan glanced back at Metcalf, her eyes razor-thin. "And what's the deal with her?"

"What do you mean?"

"Is it me, or does she seem a little too chummy with him?" Morgan asked. "They've never met before, so why is she going to bat for someone like the Witness?"

Ben forced himself to look away. He raised his sidearm to continue their perimeter search, his weak excuse for falling silent.

The truth of the matter was that Metcalf did know the Witness. Ben had found out about their connection, yet had kept the information to himself. Like so many other things of late, Ben had held back from his partner and the rest of the team.

His hope had been simple in that innocuous lie of omission. He'd wanted Metcalf to come clean on her own. This iteration of the DSA had to differ from the last. There could be no secrets. Metcalf needed to trust in them.

Ben had given Metcalf the chance for several reasons, not the least of which was the woman's connection to his deceased father. There had also been the fact that she'd saved him from a prison sentence when the Trust set him up for murder. Metcalf had given Ben a chance when no one would — or could — and he'd felt obligated to return the favor.

So far, it had not worked out for him. Morgan's probing threatened to upend everything the pair had built over the last few months. Rather than come clean to curtail permanent damage, Ben did his best to change the subject.

"What did you find?"

Morgan's brow furrowed. "What do you mean?"

"At the clinic," Ben said. "The results from my blood? Don't pretend you didn't get them."

"I did."

"Well, am I superhuman now or what?"

Morgan groaned. "Super frustrating is more like it. And by the way, nice job diverting the conversation."

"Thanks," Ben said. "You're pretty good at it, too."

"Right," she replied. Her weapon fell to her side, and she leaned against the wall. "It was clean."

"Clean?"

Morgan nodded. "No abnormalities. No signs of anything. Clean."

"Yet able to come back from the brink of death? Cool."

"Not cool," Morgan snapped. She pushed off the wall, a finger at his chest. "It explains nothing. I don't like it. And I don't like *him*."

"No one does," Ben said. The Witness stopped at the sound of their voices. He turned toward them, a sinister smirk on his face. Ben flipped him off. "Yeah, we're talking about you, Glasses."

Morgan pushed past Ben for the Witness. "What is this place, anyway? What could you possibly have been doing here?"

"Research," the Witness said. "To prepare for what's coming."

Kanigher joined them. "Cryptic much?"

"Kanigher's right," Morgan said. "We need answers. Now."

The Witness said nothing. He looked through the trio of agents toward the back of the processing room. Morgan trailed his gaze and moved toward the shadowy area.

"I'm not letting this go, you murdering son of a bitch," Morgan spat. She clicked on her flashlight, which led her through the darkened space. Ben followed closely, and Kanigher stayed behind to babysit their guest. "None of this makes any damn sense. Nothing ever does with you, and I for one am sick of—"

Her words ended abruptly. Her steps did the same, and Ben nearly collided with her.

"Ben?"

"What is it?" he asked.

"I don't want to say."

He turned on his flashlight. Following her path, the trail of light landed on what appeared to be a pillar in the room's corner. Ben didn't understand. He scanned the space, identifying two other similar structures further back. Ben stepped up to the closest one. At the first touch, Ben jumped back. His flashlight fell from his hand, hit the floor, then rolled around his feet.

"They're not pillars," he muttered. "They're—"

"Oak trees," Morgan whispered. They were broken in the center, the trunks split from within. "They've been cracked open like shells."

Ben lifted his gun toward the Witness. "What did you do?"

"Me?" The Witness made no motion to defend himself. His confident steps joined them in the room, and he flipped the switch on the adjacent wall to light up the area. "Nothing."

"These were from Bellbrook," Morgan said. "These trees were from Bellbrook."

"I told you it was merely the beginning," the Witness said. "To prepare—"

"To prepare us for what's coming," Ben finished in a mocking tone. He was tired of hearing the man's justifications. "What the hell are we doing here?"

Morgan joined Ben, weapon tight in her hand. "Answer the damn question."

"Someone has taken my subjects," the Witness said. "Someone has taken the survivors of Bellbrook."

"Taken?" Morgan scoffed. "You mean, freed them? Good. They should be so lucky."

The Witness stepped forward, his lenses reflecting their fears back on them. "And you should be concerned, Agent Dunleavy. You should be very concerned indeed."

# CHAPTER FOUR

Away from the dizzying lights of the city, and the roar of traffic on the highway, sat an innocuous complex. It took up what would have amounted to an entire block in a typical metropolis. These buildings, though, were far from civilization — east out of Millington in the nowhere town of Lakeland.

No one in the area questioned the complex. Few even realized it was there. The thick brush and the ten-foot chain-link fence certainly did their part in driving away any unwanted attention.

No signs marked the turnoff, and nothing indicated the purpose behind the complex. The lack of identification helped keep the site secure and out of the public eye. Every employee was scanned at the welcome gate, greeted by an armed guard, and then escorted to their proper parking lot. On the off-chance a visitor stumbled upon the site, the guard on duty spouted the prerequisite cover story. The business was called Signet and dealt in commercial storage for the government.

It was a half-truth. The security involved offered a glimpse at the full story. Military personnel roamed the property armed for war. Humvees drove in circles around the perimeter, a constant watch dedicated to the complex that spanned eight buildings and ten acres of land.

Signet was a government black site, though they dealt in maintaining critical records for multiple federal agencies. From Homeland Security to the Pentagon, each department held its specific secrets at Signet, and what went in rarely, if ever, left again. They were secrets few thought about, and fewer even considered when dealing with their government, which made it that much easier to keep them safe.

Few, however, ignored the rare exception to the rule. As long as one person was aware of the facility, the risk remained, and no matter the measures in place, nothing was ever guaranteed.

The problem with massive complexes came with the need to maintain personnel. Transports constantly ran into the compound. With an off-the-books military base nearby, shift changes took time to implement. The window was miniscule to observe, let alone memorize. It made for a difficult task — difficult, but not impossible.

Nothing Juniper's boss required was impossible to achieve.

She hid in the brush outside the facility. The massive forest surrounding the complex blotted out all signs of the brightening morning sky. She had been stationary for hours outside the chain-link fence, tucked away from the sensor sweeps and the intricate perimeter cameras dotting the area. Holding the same position for hours at a stretch might have made most people stiff, but not her. Just breathing in the fresh air, Juniper had never felt more alive.

Each rotation of the guards had brought more clarity to her purpose. She'd trailed the positions of the buildings and what department operated within each just by tracking the arrivals and departures. Learning which building housed her prize had been critical to her mission's success.

The master suggested stealth. It was the one sticking point in the plan she struggled against. Skulking in the shadows was how she'd lived her previous life, unassuming, and therefore passed over by those around her. Juniper refused to live that way again.

Nothing held power over her save for the master, and he trusted her to complete their objective. His request was considered and rejected. Stealth never amounted to any fun, and Juniper wanted her infiltration of the facility to be loud.

Standing from the brush, Juniper rushed for the fence. Barbed wire marked the top, adding an extra foot to the height. Her speed increased as she closed the gap from the foliage to the fence. Cameras darted in her direction, but they did not deter her approach. A Humvee caught sight of Juniper and swerved toward her position.

"What the hell is that?" one guard said. He leaped from the

vehicle, service weapon in hand.

"Looked like a woman, but—"

Juniper smiled. She was much more than a woman now. The master saw to her transformation. She owed him everything, and this was the down payment—one she was more than happy to procure for him.

Fifteen feet from the fence, Juniper launched into the air. Her incredible musculature sent her soaring through the wispy wind like an autumn leaf free from a tree.

"Holy!"

She cleared the fence, then tucked in tight for her descent. A silent nod of thanks passed to the pair of guards who had parked their Humvee right in the path of her leap. She crashed atop the roof. The chassis dented under her impact, and she rolled off the rear of the vehicle to the ground.

"How the hell did she..." the guard's question fell silent.

"Tower one, this is Hershaw," the other said into their radio. "We have an intruder. Request backup at once, and lock down the complex."

Spotlights shifted. Alarms rang out. All attention turned toward the newcomer, who remained wrapped tight in a ball.

"Don't move, lady!" The guard crept closer, mindful of the sweat coating his hands as he gripped tight to his firearm.

Juniper didn't bother to listen. She stood, unhurt and unafraid.

"I said—"

She grabbed the barrel of the weapon. The speed of her motion shocked the guard. He failed to depress the trigger, the moment gone in the blink of an eye. Juniper pulled the man toward her with one hand. The other caught him by the neck. One quick jerk and a hardy snap ended the soldier's life.

"My God," Hershaw muttered. It was the last thing he ever said. Juniper pounced at the man. Shots erupted, yet none hit their mark. She slapped the gun aside. The force broke the man's trigger finger. Before he could cry out in pain, she grabbed his head and slammed him onto the pavement.

More guards closed in on her position. A smile greeted them. She thrilled at the exhilaration of the fight, and the pleasure that came with extreme violence from those who sought to keep her from her prize.

Juniper ducked out of the line of fire, sweeping toward the closest building. She dove between jeeps and SUVs that carried government plates. Each plate carried the Signet name, followed by a two-digit number to identify the vehicle in the lot.

Bullets followed her every movement. A stray shot caught the fuel tank of the SUV to her left.

The explosion ripped through the complex. Juniper soared forward; the shockwave caused her to crash into the side of the building. By the time she found her feet again, six guards surrounded her.

"This ends now," one announced.

"Don't you dare move!" another one shouted.

Juniper raised her hands. She interlocked her fingers behind her head. She sensed their approach, slow and cautious. Their wariness was well-advised, but also afforded her the time she required to find the window she'd been searching for in the building. She crouched down, and the approach of the guards paused for a second.

The delay cost them. Juniper bounded for the third-floor window and crashed inside the building. She rolled with the landing, then jumped to her feet.

"What the hell?" a woman cried from behind her desk.

"Breach!" another yelled. "We've been breached!"

It was a records room. Four desks, one in each corner, kept the records in question directly between them. The four keepers shot to their feet, weapons in hand. They were unaccustomed to action, yet their training suited them well.

Bullets cut through the room. Juniper ducked under the first barrage, and two of the women took each other out in the crossfire. The second pair were luckier, and the guards from outside joined them in their fight.

Juniper closed the gap on the squad. She needed time, and if they would not provide any for her, she would simply take it. Bodies collapsed under her blows. People screamed, but their cries fell on deaf ears. They stood in her way and paid for it with their lives.

When Juniper's vision cleared, blood ran in thick globs from her knuckles. Her clothing was torn, yet no apparent injuries decorated her flawless skin.

"You... you killed them all," a demure young woman said

from behind her desk. She lifted her weapon and fired. Fear caused her to close her eyes.

The bullet pierced Juniper's shoulder. She did not falter from the impact. The smile, the rush from her actions, mellowed. Juniper lifted the closest corpse. Secure in her tight grip, she tossed the body at the armed woman. Bones snapped in the collision and the woman fell.

Juniper rounded the desk, then stepped over the body to view her struggling victim beneath. The records keeper reached for her weapon, to no avail. Juniper stared, curious at the woman's struggle. Slowly, she lifted her foot over the woman's face and brought it down hard.

Alarms continued to blare outside. The sound of rushed steps ran through the corridors of the building. Juniper slammed the door shut. She clicked the lock, then started in on the records.

A quick search provided her with the paperwork and IDs her master required. His research was a thorough enough guide to make the process easy. That was the first part of the mission. From there, Juniper started for the bodies on the ground. She sized them up and stripped the appropriate soldier of their uniform. Quickly donning the stolen clothing, Juniper gathered up her belongings. IDs slipped into her pockets, the records tucked securely under her arm. A set of keys joined the ill-gotten goods, lifted from the chain near the door. The fob attached was marked with a red 13.

Outside the room, security filled the hall. Their shadows ran beneath the door frame. They would breach within seconds. Instead of preparing for another fight, Juniper headed for the window.

The moment the first soldier stepped foot in the room, Juniper jumped out of the third-story window. She held tight to the records and the keys. Her feet hit the pavement, and she started for the parking lot.

Shots rang out from above. More rose in the distance. The guards scrambled for her position. Juniper raced for the vehicle marked SIGNET-13 in the lot and ducked inside. It started up immediately, and she barreled from the spot toward the front gate.

Soldiers dove out of the way at her approach. They fired, but their shots were wasted; they attempted to wound instead of ending the threat the way she had been taught. Juniper seized on their hesitancy. The transport slammed through the barricades, tore through the fence, and reached the empty road beyond.

Satisfied at her escape, Juniper tapped the communication device nestled in her right ear. "I have what is required."

"Good work," the master replied. His enthusiasm brought a smile to her face. "The rendezvous is in one hour. Make haste, my dear."

"On my way."

# CHAPTER FIVE

Zac Modine woke in a strange place. It was becoming a nightmarish theme in his life: the apparent disconnect from reality. The last thing he remembered was Arcadia. He had left Adler at the diner. Their conversation had not gone well, but her mention of a signal had ignited a million thoughts in his mind.

He'd left her for the trail through the Ozarks. It had been his getaway, a place to think without the buzzing sound in the back of his mind. Yet, when he had reached the trail, something had stopped him.

Zac sat up in bed and rubbed his neck. He closed his eyes, trying to remember. *What was it? What happened next?*

There had been three unmarked vehicles. SUVs had headed for the bed-and-breakfast he'd been staying at during his time in Arcadia. Zac had taken the sign and rushed to his room. His bag had remained packed the entire time, so there had been nothing to do but grab his gear. Beyond his swift departure, there was nothing left to recall.

His memory was blank.

Zac pulled back his unkempt hair, then moved to the side of the bed. It was a motel, for sure. Second-hand tables and lamps rested in front of a pair of closed burgundy curtains that were frayed in multiple sections. The dresser was notched, as if moved several times from multiple domiciles over the years—another thrift shop discovery. Even the bed appeared in disrepair; the frame wobbly at the merest touch.

The sound of the road outside roared through the shoddy windows. Turning to the nightstand, Zac noticed leaflets piled up under the lamp. He lifted the top one; the destination listed in bold letters forced all exhaustion from his eyes.

"Nebraska?" he exclaimed, nearly dropping the flyer. It read GRAND ISLAND and showed the image of a local festival with families laughing and playing. "What the hell am I doing in Nebraska?"

He threw the leaflet to the ground, then stood. Stretching, Zac's body struggled through the aches and pains of a long rest. His mind was still a cloud, the effects of the missing time continued to wreak havoc with his senses. Hurried steps carried him across the room to the bathroom. When he turned the corner of the bed, however, Zac's toes slammed into the side of a large metal obstruction on the floor.

"Dammit!" He cradled the stubbed toes, cursing wildly at the instrument of his pain. Stumbling back to the side of the bed, Zac stared at the apparatus. "What the hell is this now?"

At the onset of the question, Zac cried out in pain. His agony came not from his collision with the mechanism on the floor, but from his temples. He dropped his toes and gripped tight to the sides of his head. Falling from the bed, Zac curled into a ball. His scream echoed through the room as visions danced behind his eyelids.

Thousands of images flooded his mind. Schematics laid out before him as if handmade, like they had been designed and built up layer by layer through his thoughts. Every intake valve, every cylinder, every belt loop, and wiring configuration. He went through every iteration, every failed test and breakthrough, in a matter of seconds.

After the images passed, Zac opened his eyes. He recognized the apparatus immediately: a car engine. While not as refined as the schematics downloaded to his brain, it was modeled on the product he pictured in his mind's eye. Instead of high-end manufactured parts, it had been built with scraps from a junkyard or collected from dumpsters.

"How?" he asked to the silence of the room. Zac circled the engine, noting the parameters set within his mind. It was a clean engine, with no carbon footprint to speak of—something still being tested in several countries without a timeline of release. "How did I build this? How long have I been out of it?"

"Nearly two days," a voice answered.

Zac spun to greet the newcomer to the conversation. Where

once his reflection greeted him in the mirror across from the bed, a woman's face took over. April Newton offered him a sad smile.

"You," Zac seethed. He closed his eyes again to wish her image away. When he opened them, her presence remained. In truth, she had been with him every moment since they'd met. She had died in his arms; her last act had transferred her consciousness to him. "You took over for two days?"

"The programming did, yes," she replied matter-of-factly. "You were in danger. It was a safety measure."

"I wasn't in danger," Zac snapped. "I had my bag in hand. I was on my way out."

"Not fast enough," April said.

"Fine." Zac refused to look in the mirror. He focused on the engine at his feet. "Then explain the last two days. Getting me out of Arcadia is one thing, but this?"

"The pressure built up, Zac. Your mind needed a release from the accumulated knowledge stored inside you. It will only become worse the more you fight the programming."

"So I should just give up my life?" he said to the image of April in the mirror. "Why not, right? The world would probably be better off without me, anyway."

Zac found his bag tucked in the corner. He pulled out a pair of jeans and a less-than-fresh t-shirt. A quick change and Zac started for the door.

"Where are you going?"

"Away from this."

"You can't keep running."

Zac's hand fell from the handle. He stared deep into the mirror. "*I'm* not doing anything, it seems."

"Zac..."

"Don't," he said. A set of keys sat on the dresser before the mirror. They rested atop a rental agreement, his signature on the document, yet he held no memory of the exchange. Zac grimaced, then snatched up the keys. "And I'm not running. I'm trying to make things right for... for..."

Horror filled him. The name escaped him. The silence that came with trying to recall his wife's name staggered him. Zac tumbled back to the bed. He tried to picture her face, to hear her voice, but the memories caused the pain to return.

Zac spun toward the mirror, eyes pleading with the image in

the glass. April's gaze fell low with shame.

"Claire."

His chest unclenched. His pulse slowed. *Claire. How the hell could I forget Claire?*

"That's right," he said with false confidence. "And Alex."

"It's getting more difficult to remember," April said.

Zac slammed his hands against the dresser. "So help me!"

"I…"

"The signal," he said. She had mentioned it in passing before. So had Adler. Zac believed it to be the key to his salvation. "Where is it?"

"I'm sorry, Zac." Her image faded from the mirror.

"No!" he shouted. "Don't you dare—"

She disappeared, and only his reflection remained. Zac stared into his worn eyes, bloodshot and pained. He waited for her return, for some sign that she understood and sympathized with his plight, but April hid from view.

Defeated, Zac stomped from the room. Daylight greeted him, the sun blazing overhead. The humidity slammed into him, and his shirt glommed tight to his skin. Hitting the lock button on his keys, a mid-size sedan beeped a greeting.

Zac headed for the car and hopped inside. He backed out slowly from the lot. It had been a long time since he'd driven anywhere. It felt great to do something normal. With each passing mile marker, calm swept over him.

It was the first time he truly felt like Zac again, and not some program. He needed to erase the Wellspring consciousness from his mind. He needed to be free of the protocol stealing his entire existence away. The signal was the key to that freedom, and the only way he could get his life back. The signal was his only chance to make amends with Claire and Alex.

Zac continued to repeat their names during his drive. Shops and restaurants filled the strip surrounding the motel. He journeyed north, deeper into the downtown area. Retail was a dominant factor in the district, but more offices and high rises took root. Noting an IHOP three miles into his trip, Zac left the road and found a parking spot in front.

It wasn't until he stepped outside that he noticed them: the company he'd picked up since the motel. Eyes were on him from multiple directions, but Zac tried to remain oblivious. He tinkered with the door. Pretending to have trouble with the locking mechanism gave him time to scan the block.

A gray sedan parked on the street, two shadows prominent in the front seat. A pair of pedestrians rested along the corner of the building. They stretched from a recent run, but they weren't sweating at all.

"Is it them?" Zac asked quietly.

April's face reflected off the driver's-side window. "Yes."

"Don't take over," he said. "Just tell me what to do."

"Run, Zac. You have to run now."

# CHAPTER SIX

"I need a hand with this," Morgan called. Her hands were deep in the oak's trunk. Fluid dripped from her fingers, and she fought to keep her mouth closed. Ben hesitated a moment to join her.

"What's up?" he asked, wincing at the goop dripping from his partner's hands. "What have you found?"

"More than I thought possible," Morgan muttered. "But that isn't really a surprise with this guy, is it?"

The Witness maintained his distance. He leaned casually along a processing machine in the center of the floor. His gaze appeared to remain locked on them at all times, but being unable to see his eyes made it difficult to confirm. Their unwelcome guest offered little in the way of answers, instead allowing Morgan to investigate the questions herself, which left the rest of the team twiddling their thumbs.

Metcalf and Kanigher joined the pair of agents at the tree. Morgan pulled back at their approach. Her hands held tight to a thick cord from within the cavernous trunk.

"That…"

"Smells terrible," Kanigher finished for their superior. Both pinched their noses but remained close to keep their voices down.

"It's like an umbilical cord." Morgan nodded to Ben, who lifted his flashlight into the shadowy space. "Take a look for yourself. This tree sustained a life inside it. This cord and these filaments embedded themselves in the skin to feed the occupant enough nutrients and oxygen to keep them alive."

"How?" Metcalf asked. "How is something like this possible?"

"It isn't," Morgan replied. She opened a small case at her side to reveal a portable lab kit. Slides and a microscope sat inside, along with several empty specimen containers. "It *shouldn't* be possible, at any rate. Of course, I've said the same damn thing way too much since Bellbrook."

It always came back to Bellbrook. A renegade signal transformed the population of the town. Seven thousand people were turned into trees and believed lost. The government had certainly seemed to think so. They had burned much of the forest in the aftermath. Ben believed it all to be lost, the same as the Spring Hill site.

The Witness, however, knew things differently.

Ben left the group to their discussion. They continued to murmur their findings. Questions circled among them, yet they found no concrete answers. Ben had his own to explore and took the opportunity.

"Can I help you, Agent Riley?"

"Yeah." He grabbed the sleeve of the Witness' jacket and dragged him away from the others, deeper into the processing area of the lumber mill. "You can start sharing with the class."

"I brought you here, didn't I?"

"Leading us by the nose, yet backing away when we have something to talk about?" Ben asked. "How do you think that's going to end?"

"I know very well how things will end," the mysterious man answered.

"Right," Ben said. "Because you've seen it. That's what I'm supposed to believe, at any rate."

The Witness peered back at the group, then leaned closer to Ben. "That is what Wesley Fuller told you, isn't it?"

Ben's eyes lit up. Of course, he knew about their exchange and the secrets shared by the former DSA agent. "You are him, aren't you? Joshua Falk?"

"A name lost to time."

"I don't get it," Ben continued. "If you're him... if you're actually one of us, even from way back then, why aren't you willing to stand with us? Why haven't you just told us what we need to do to stop what's coming? What are you so afraid of?"

"It doesn't work like that," the Witness said. "Take too active a hand, and you lose sight of the bigger picture. You handle a single case, you tackle a lone problem, and claim victory without realizing the ten other defeats you've suffered in your ignorance."

"Says the man unwilling to enlighten us," Ben snapped. "This place, for instance."

"Abandoned and well-suited to my needs."

"To do what?" Ben asked. "What were you doing here?"

The Witness turned to the rest of the group. "They required further study."

"They were people." Spit flew from Ben's lips. "They had families and lives. You killed them."

"No," the Witness shot back. "The Department of Defense burned them to the ground. I sought to save them."

"Three?" Ben pointed to the trunks in the back room. "Three out of how many?"

The Witness shook his head and started for the others. Ben took hold of his sleeve once more.

"Ruth Heller died in that forest."

Head bowed, the enigmatic traveler refused to look at the angry agent. "She needn't have, Benjamin. That was not how her story should have ended."

Ben clenched his fist. He wanted to tear into the Witness, to unleash all his anger and fury. Letting it all fall away, Ben pushed through the Witness for the rest of the group.

"Like I can believe a word you say."

"You should," the Witness replied. "Part of you does. That is why you haven't shared my name with the rest."

"That isn't—"

"After all I've done for you, I would hope for a small degree of courtesy," the Witness continued. "A modicum of faith in my sincerity."

"Never. Going. To happen."

"Very well." The Witness tucked his hands into the pockets of his coat and returned to the back room. "Then allow me to corroborate Agent Dunleavy's findings."

All three stopped their work on the trunk. Morgan let the cord go. She wiped the fluid from her hands on the base of the trunk. Kanigher continued to hold tight to his sidearm, a constant eye on their company. Metcalf, however, was more focused on Ben—clearly concerned over their private chat.

Ben wanted to say more. He wanted to do more to the man. One look at Morgan stopped him short of acting. She shook her head, obviously willing to listen to the Witness' claims, especially after what she found within the carcass of the tree.

The Witness cleared his throat. "The signal used in Bellbrook and Spring Hill forced the host body inert. The tree that formed around them acted as little more than a chrysalis."

"Why?" Morgan asked, unsatisfied with the man's explanation. "For what purpose?"

"To evolve," the Witness said. "To force a second stage on humanity."

He moved for the tree trunk. "This was all meant to be a preventative measure. Designed by Howard Clevinger, and disseminated by me, for the sole purpose of safeguarding the world."

Ben's chuckle filled the air, quieting the excited Witness. "We're not really listening to this, are we?" He pulled out his sidearm and lifted it toward the murderer. "You know what? I'm not. Not anymore."

Metcalf cut between them, cold eyes digging deep. "Put it down, Riley."

Ben shook his head. His finger tightened on the trigger.

"Don't, Ben."

Ben's brow furrowed. "Morgan?"

She sighed, clearly frustrated at her decision. "He's not lying. The people weren't dead, not by his hand anyway. If this one is any indication, with the material I've found and the systems feeding its occupant, there is every reason to believe the people survived their transformation."

"You can't—"

Morgan stood and moved for him. Her hand settled on his weapon to lower it, but her eyes never left his. "There's blood inside. Human blood. It will take me time to analyze it, but from what little I've been able to tell, it's unlike anything I've ever seen before. A whole new cell structure, with antibodies beyond belief.

"I know you want to hurt him for what he did," Morgan continued. "I feel the same. And he will absolutely pay when this is over. But he's not lying about this, Ben."

"I'm glad someone can see reason on this team," the Witness

said with a smile. "I appreciate the assistance, Agent Dunleavy."

"Shove your appreciation," Morgan snapped. "You are the reason Ruth Heller and Lincoln MacKenzie are no longer with us. Not the Department of Defense, and not Greg Sullivan. They are dead because of you."

"Two lives in the face of billions?"

Morgan snatched the man's collar and squeezed. "You don't get to justify this!"

"That's enough." Metcalf sidled up to Morgan. Her hand fell atop her compatriots, and Morgan let go of the man. Morgan stomped away for the tree. Lincoln's death was still a raw wound for her. Metcalf, however, tried to move past the confrontation. "So what happened?"

"A mistake," the Witness explained. "With the death of the Wellspring, I stepped away from my research. Her loss was a blow to the Trust, and I sought to exploit it. I didn't realize how long I had been gone."

Ben smirked at the remark. "Time slipped away from you."

The Witness' empty gaze locked on Ben. "Suffice it to say, when I returned I found this."

"It's only three people," Kanigher said. "How much damage could they do?"

"Your associate noted their cell structure, Agent Kanigher." The Witness ran his hand along the trunk with pride. "Their skin is dense, their bodies invulnerable to pain. They carry increased strength from the change. Yet, they have the maturity of a newborn."

"Controllable assets," Metcalf said.

"I'm afraid so."

"Someone took them," Kanigher commented.

"Someone had to," the Witness confirmed. "They were incapable of independent thought."

"Who?"

"I don't know." Metcalf's cold gaze met the Witness' words with disbelief. He didn't flinch from her. "That is why I came to you. No one knew of this place. No one knows about me."

"I..." Ben started to speak, then thought better of it. He had kept his knowledge of the Witness to himself since discovering the truth about the man's identity, unsure how to proceed. Morgan turned at the sound of his voice, curious about what was on his mind. He merely shook his head and took a step back.

"So we don't have a single clue where to look," Kanigher said in frustration. The rest joined his feeling with a shared grumble of discontent. "Perfect."

# CHAPTER SEVEN

The arguments from inside the lumber mill filled the computer's internal speakers. Heated words echoed through the cabin of the van, but none affected the occupants. Adler knew where the anger came from for her companions. Their passion for the mission, and their desire to help, fueled their lives. It was why she joined them in the aftermath of Sullivan's coup, and why she believed in them so fiercely.

Ben's frustration came from the losses he suffered in Buffalo. The deaths of Lincoln, Grissom, and so many others plagued Morgan's memory. Metcalf was simply angry all the time. Kanigher was the oddity in the bunch, willing to remain professional no matter how many jokes Ben uttered, or how many secrets were kept by Metcalf.

Adler had studied them all. Their time in the Bunker might have been boring to the others, but it gave her time to connect with them, to see them for more than the butt-kicking task force known as the DSA, and as the people they truly were. They were people Adler respected. As their cheerleader and their confidant, she always hoped to do her best on their behalf.

Nixon remained a complete and total mystery to her, though. He swigged his Pepsi, his third bottle of the day, while maintaining total focus on the monitors in the van. He scanned radio broadcasts, police bands, as well as traffic copters for signs of trouble. No one asked this of him — in fact, no one asked much from Nixon for the mission. He merely took it upon himself to dive in.

Adler appreciated his company in that regard. It caused her to drop her own task, that of thermal readings from inside the lumber mill, to stare at the man's work habits. She couldn't help but find him fascinating, like a lab experiment.

His nervous ticks were well-hidden, yet poked through. There was the way he tapped his foot in rhythm to his typing and the way he jotted down random thoughts between tasks—more work to take up instead of succumbing to simple human needs like sleep. She wondered if he had a cognitive disorder that only hacking seemed to abate for a time, or if he was as brilliant as he acted.

Nixon turned to toss his latest soda. A curious look spread on his face at Adler's staring, and his cheeks flushed.

"What?" He pulled his headphones down around his neck. "Do I have something on my face?"

"No," Adler said with a whimsy wave. "I was—"

"Cause I was eating some peanut butter earlier, and it always sticks to the corners," Nixon interrupted. He swiped at his lips. Unsatisfied with his success, Nixon dipped into his go-bag beneath the monitor station. "I brought some wipes just in case. I know they're here somewhere."

Adler left her station. Her hand fell on his. "Your face is fine." She smiled, and her nose scrunched up. "Besides the nervous sweating going on now."

"What?" Nixon bounded up from his chair and slammed into the roof of the van. "Ow."

"Are you—"

"Fine." He rubbed at the back of his head. "I'm fine."

"I didn't mean to—"

"No, no." He crashed into his seat. "I should have been more chatty. Seems to be a thing with this team."

"Like a big ol' dysfunctional family," Adler confirmed with a nod.

"So, this is standard?" Nixon asked. "Our role?"

Adler spread her arms. "Support status in all its glory. At least they asked us along this time, instead of leaving us behind."

"After the shootout I endured with Susan the other night, I think I prefer the Bunker," Nixon said. "Plenty to keep me busy there, and less chance of the whole dying-in-the-line-of-duty thing."

"Right."

"The van's nice, though," Nixon said, clearly reading her disappointment. "And the company helps."

"I was thinking the same thing."

His hand fell to his neck, awkwardly rubbing the back of his headphones instead of his skin. "Oh, I...," he muttered. The confidence left him, and the sputtering of a young man took over. "Well, Alison, maybe we could—"

"What's that?"

"Well, I was trying to say that if you wanted to, not that you have to, but if you wanted to, we could..." Nixon reached for her hand. Adler, however, shuffled past him for the monitor station. "Wait, what?"

"There's something on your screen. How do I—" She disconnected the headphone jack. Radio calls on the police band drowned out the sound of the field team. "There."

Nixon wheeled back into position. Adler shifted aside to give him room. "Let me see."

"Your station, your rules," Adler replied.

"Not at all," Nixon said. The confidence that came from the work returned and took over from the awkwardness of his earlier sputtering. She let his question die out, giving him a reprieve. "I was monitoring local chatter, checking any hotspots that might indicate a potential threat. See if we could figure out who was to blame for what's going on inside the mill."

"It was a good idea, Nixon."

"I'm sure anyone would have done the same."

"Take the compliment."

Nixon nodded. "Got it. Thanks."

"This is the police band?" Adler asked.

"No," Nixon said. "Hang on."

He slipped the headphone jack into place, and the sound quieted down. Adler was left with the team's comm chirping in her ear. She threw him a dissatisfied glance.

"Sorry." He pressed tight to the headphone. "I needed a better listen."

"Got it."

Silence took hold for a moment. Nixon leaned forward in the chair, his brow furrowed in confusion.

"It's not the police," he said. "Frequency reads military. A government black site."

"Something happened?"

Nixon nodded, then removed the headphones. "You're going to want to hear this. So will the rest of the team. I think I found who they're looking for."

# CHAPTER EIGHT

Metcalf cursed under her breath. This wasn't working out. She'd known it the moment the Witness had entered the Bunker. There had been no doubt in her mind what the reaction from the team would be; their hatred of the man had been evident ever since Bellbrook.

Hers had grown from that event, but for an entirely different reason. That was the sticking point, one which Ben made self-evident with every glare in her direction. He had called her out on her prior knowledge of the Witness, a relationship she had kept secret for years until needing his help to save Ben's life. It had been the right decision, but she had paid for it since then.

That had been her reasoning behind keeping the secret in the first place: the reaction of the team. Everything she did served to hold the DSA together and maintain the mission above all else. When the Witness had requested their assistance, Metcalf had promised to handle the situation without his presence. The Witness had balked at the suggestion.

Incredibly, Nixon had agreed with the Witness. His defiance in the face of his superior had grated her to no end, but his threat of outing the Witness to the others could not be ignored. The new recruit hated secrets, something she should have realized from his past.

Having the enigmatic man in the field with the rest of the team drove a wedge into their dynamic. Tension refused to abate, which led to arguing over the innate trust they once held for each other. Or, at least, the trust they held for everyone except her.

She earned their doubts after what happened to the former

DSA. Metcalf, however, could no longer afford to consider them — not with their current predicament.

"Thoughts?" The question silenced the grumbling of the others. They stood near the open tree trunk, their main specimen and piece of evidence of the Bellbrook affair. The Witness stayed away from the impromptu meeting. He had read the situation well enough to realize his opinion was no longer warranted or desired.

Ben spoke up first. It was his way and always would be, no matter how many times it bit him in the ass. "We walk away. No question."

"What?" Metcalf shot back. "Riley, that's not an option."

"He's manipulating us," Ben said. "He has been from the beginning."

"He's not the only one," Kanigher muttered under his breath. His arms crossed his chest. Stark brown eyes stared deep at Metcalf.

"Bobby?" Surprise filled her voice. Out of everyone in the room, she always believed Kanigher to be on her side over all others. Yet, his sparse verbal jabs since their arrival at the lumber mill made her question his position.

"When were you going to tell us?" he asked.

"About what?"

Kanigher pointed at the Witness. "How long have you known this guy?"

"I…" Metcalf bit back her answer. She shook her head and turned away rather than face the nods of agreement rising from Morgan.

"He just pops up during your op, and you roll out the red carpet?" Kanigher pressed.

"Kanigher's right," Morgan chimed in. Her ego refused to let go of a fight. "After Bellbrook, I thought we were all on the same page about the Witness. He was persona non grata. The big, bad monster. You've been lying to us for months, Metcalf."

She hesitated to respond. Every instinct screamed for her to lie. Ben's knowing stare demanded the truth, no matter what fight might occur.

"I had to," she said, facing her accusers once more. "You don't understand what he is. What he's doing here."

"Ben?" Morgan turned to her partner, concern on her face.

"You're awfully quiet."

"He knew," Kanigher commented with a scoff.

Shock broke out in Morgan's face. Her hands dropped to her sides, her brow furrowed. "Did you?"

Ben's gaze fell.

"How could you not say a word?"

"I was hoping she would," Ben replied. "I was wrong."

Morgan's fists clenched. "This man killed Ruth, Metcalf! You sent Lincoln after him! Was that to cover up your guilt?"

"Yes, dammit!" Metcalf shouted. Everyone fell back a step at her confession. "I didn't know about Bellbrook ahead of time. I didn't know his intentions would go so far. After what he did? I wanted him dead."

Ben huffed. "For using you like you do everyone else. You're a piece of work."

Morgan shook her head. Anger radiated from her as she paced around the group in a circle. "I agree with Ben. We walk away."

"No," Metcalf said. "The Witness is too important. He's a valuable asset."

"That's all we are to you, aren't we?" Kanigher asked, disgust in his voice.

"Bobby, you have to understand," she said. Metcalf hated how much his words stung, but she swallowed the feeling as she did with everything else. There simply wasn't the time for it. "This is the mission."

"*Your* mission," he snapped. "We're all collateral damage to be used and bartered when you see fit."

"That's not true, I—"

The comm line chirped. Tension settled between them at the sound. The physical distance of the group seemed to widen with each accusation, to where they were spread throughout the back room of the lumber mill.

Metcalf felt the cold of the room in that moment, grateful for the slight reprieve from Adler's voice in her ear.

"Sorry to interrupt."

"Go ahead, Adler," Metcalf said. "It's fine."

"Nixon found something of interest," Adler continued. "I'm patching it to your phone."

Metcalf took out the small device. It began to play the uploaded content immediately. "What am I looking at?"

"It started on the military feeds," Adler said. "A black site was infiltrated. Heavy casualties. They tried to keep it hush-hush, but when things go boom, people tend to notice. Looks like the media got hold of it, and are now at the scene."

Metcalf opened up the video link to a live broadcast. A female reporter spoke in the background as smoke and ash from a raging fire filled the feed.

"—where eyewitnesses describe the woman as capable of leaping over a ten-foot fence and shattering concrete in her hands," the reporter said. "The devastation is clear at the Signet facility. But who was this woman, and how was she able to achieve such incredible feats? More details as they—"

"It's them."

All turned to see the Witness standing beside them. No emotion entered his summation, no anger at the loss of his precious experiment. There was only the cold realization that his mistake was out in the open. People were dying because of it.

"One of yours?" Morgan said.

"Yes."

Metcalf tucked the phone in her pocket, then pointed for the door. "We need to move."

No one took a single step. Suspicious glances passed between the team, their doubts almost palpable. Each waited for someone to take the lead, to speak up, or to follow the command of the woman who was supposed to be their superior.

Metcalf cut between them. "We can continue this later."

Kanigher dropped his hands to his sides, then offered a slight nod. He brushed past the Witness before heading for the exit. Ben followed along. His hand hovered over his sidearm with every glimpse of the Witness.

Morgan was the last to move. She looked back at the tree trunks, the gift left for them by the Witness, and the cost of trusting the man for even a second.

"Morgan…" Metcalf started. The second her voice hit the air, Morgan spun to greet her—fury in her eyes.

"This isn't over, Metcalf," Morgan said. "Not by a long shot."

Metcalf waited for the steps to fall into the background. She swiped at her eyes, wishing she didn't understand what Morgan meant with her words. But she knew the truth.

This was just beginning.

# CHAPTER NINE

"Kanigher and I will take point on this."

The orders started flying the second they vacated the lumber mill. Metcalf cut them off from the two vehicles that had brought them to the facility. An immediate groan escaped Morgan upon hearing her voice.

This wasn't the time for orders. This sure as hell wasn't the time for Metcalf to be issuing anything but damn apologies, but that was never going to happen.

"You two stay here and coordinate with Nixon and Adler," Metcalf continued. "Relay any information you find, and we'll handle it. We'll call as soon as we know what happened at the black site."

"We should all go," Morgan said.

"There is still plenty to learn here," Metcalf shot back. "My call."

"It always is."

"No one mentioned Glasses." Ben pointed to their unwanted guest. "Is he part of the Blue or Gold team in this equation?"

Blank stares met his comment. Morgan pushed through them. "It's an *X-Men* reference. Forget it. Ben does have a point."

"I do?"

Morgan rolled her eyes. "For once, yes." She turned to Metcalf. "He's not staying with us."

Kanigher leaned in. "It's a government site. Taking him is a bad idea."

"Yet, he's already made his choice clear," Metcalf said. The Witness sat in the back seat of the first van, ready for departure. He tossed them a wave and a smile.

Morgan nearly screamed. His very presence set her off, but the fact that Metcalf bent over backward for the man threatened to send her over the edge. "Kanigher's right, Metcalf, and you know it."

"Debate time is over," Metcalf snapped. "I don't like it any more than you do."

"Doubtful," Morgan muttered.

Metcalf caught the comment. Refusing to engage, she turned to Kanigher, then tilted her head at the waiting car. "Let's get this over with."

"Have fun," Ben called after them.

"We'll keep you in the loop," Metcalf said. "Be sure to do the same."

Morgan remained quiet. Being in the loop required trust, something that was impossible with Metcalf. She thought things had changed in the wake of the DSA's fall. She was wrong to believe Metcalf could change, wrong to think the mission came second to their lives.

Adler and Nixon stepped out of the van as the others left the lot. "What did we miss?"

Nixon's eyebrow shot up at Adler's question. "We didn't miss anything. We were listening the whole—"

Adler shot out her elbow and clipped the tech on the arm.

"Ow," Nixon exclaimed, rubbing at the wound. He clearly read her look, then nodded. "Right. We didn't hear a thing. Got it."

"Monitor the feeds," Morgan said. She found it easier to talk with Adler and Nixon. She wondered if Metcalf would ruin the trust between them as well. "The media might have caught wind of the event, but that doesn't mean the military is going to be in a sharing mood. Keep an ear on any chatter, and we'll be ready to move at a moment's notice."

"We're on it," Adler confirmed.

Nixon hesitated for a second, stretching from their time in the van. Adler, however, grabbed him by the arm and pulled him back toward the van. The side door slid shut behind them.

"Want to talk about it?" Ben asked.

What she wanted to do was wipe the smirk off his face. It had no right to be present, not after everything she had seen in the lumber mill or heard from her so-called colleagues. Instead,

Morgan attempted to rein in her anger.

"You didn't tell me about Metcalf."

"Like I said, I was hoping Metcalf would do the talking."

"Coming from you, that's a surprise. You love the sound of your own voice."

Ben sighed. "Look, I get being mad at me."

"Oh, I'm way past mad. You held back vital intel, and I get the feeling there's more you're not saying. What were you talking about in there with the Witness, anyway?"

Ben refused to meet her gaze. "Nothing."

"Yeah." Morgan shook her head. "Like I said. Holding back."

"Morgan—"

"This doesn't work if I don't know what's going on." Morgan pushed through him for the mill. "Don't be like Metcalf, Ben. That path only leads to misery."

"That's not what I want, Morgan."

"Yet, it's what you're choosing." Her words were tinged with sadness and disappointment. "My equipment is still inside. I'm going to take a closer look at those specimens while I have a minute."

"I'll join you."

"No," she replied brusquely. "I'd rather you didn't."


A circus surrounded the facility. The entire road was a hazard: cars blocked every lane and lined up for a mile on either side. Metcalf worked the van through the cordons and past the encamped media. The occupants of the van kept their heads down to stay out of the limelight. The last thing they needed was attention, especially with their guest in the back.

Once through the main obstruction, Metcalf parked where instructed. Kanigher showed off their credentials to gain access, happy to help but unwilling to say a damn word to Metcalf the entire drive over. Metcalf wondered whether the same held true for the rest of the team, if they could even call themselves that after finding out her dirty little secret.

Metcalf tossed their passenger a knowing stare. The Witness read her intent very well and settled deeper into the fabric of the seat. Still, she felt the need to reiterate the command.

"Stay here."

Kanigher turned at her words. "Are you sure?"

Metcalf reached for the handle and opened the door. The cool wind was comforting, and she quickly embraced it. Kanigher joined her seconds later, constantly aware of the man they had left behind.

"Susan…"

Metcalf shook her head. "I don't want to hear it right now."

Kanigher sped up and blocked her from the entrance to the complex. "You need to."

She pushed through him for the gate. Security surrounded the fence. Behind them, Metcalf noticed the smoke still rising from the fires in the parking lot and the overturned vehicles.

"Stop," Kanigher called. "Just stop."

She did, and her head sank to her chest. Spinning on her heels, Metcalf started for Kanigher. He took a step back to give her room, but she continued until she was in his face.

"I have a rogue experiment on the loose, Bobby," she said through clenched teeth. "I can only deal with one crisis at a time."

"Then stop creating new ones." She shook her head in defiance, and Kanigher pressed the issue harder. "These people need you to trust them. You think they wanted to give up their lives, any chance at normality, for an extended stay at Chez Bunker?"

"No one asked them to—"

"Yes, you did!" Kanigher shot back. "Repeatedly. You… you don't even see it."

"See what?"

"How you manipulate them. How you hold back or outright lie."

"I don't." The rebuttal was weak. The lie was too apparent for both of them.

"How long have you known him, Susan?" Kanigher asked in a soft voice. It was the voice of a concerned friend, not a jilted colleague. "How long have you been working with the Witness?"

She didn't offer a reply. Part of her wanted to come clean, to make up for the lies and the secrets. The rest of her demanded both stay locked inside for as long as possible. That was where they were safe. It was how Metcalf had survived through the years. She didn't know any other way to be.

"Nothing?" Kanigher said, unsurprised. He moved for the gate. "Yeah, that's what I thought."

"It's complicated."

Kanigher shook his head, then pointed for the van. "He's a confessed murderer. What we like to call the bad guy. Not that complicated."

There was no answer to give him. Nothing she said made up for the lie she had carried for so long. The truth no longer mattered at the moment, not with a man like the Witness, and not when it came to her reasons for holding back from the team.

Kanigher's hands fell to his hips. Metcalf never thought he would turn on her, never question her judgment about their work. She thought he knew her best and would always be by her side. It hurt her to see him this way — as aggravated as the rest... and as betrayed.

"The team won't wait for an answer," Kanigher said. "They need the truth. All of it. Or do you want to see your precious DSA fall apart again?"

She heard every word. The conversation had played out in her mind dozens of times before. She knew it by heart, yet she continued to make the wrong choice.

Metcalf offered him a nod. "After the mission."

Kanigher caught her by the arm when she tried to pass. "Susan."

"After." She yanked loose from his grip. "Now follow my lead."

"No way," Kanigher said. "I've got this."

"I'm in command here, Bobby, so cut the crap."

Kanigher scoffed. "And I thought I had followed you long enough for some trust, but I guess I was wrong. About a lot of things, it seems."

She wanted to scream. Even a simple move had become complicated by the lack of trust in her. The team couldn't afford to falter — not now, and not with the Witness among them. Metcalf glanced back at their van. Her eyes widened at the emptiness inside.

"Wait," she called to Kanigher. "Where's the Witness?"

Frantically, both looked around. Desperate to find their missing guest, they scanned the parking lot, to no avail. When they spun back to the facility, they saw him standing on the opposite side of the fence.

The Witness gestured them over. "You two coming?"

Kanigher's hand shot to his sidearm. "I swear to God."

Metcalf stopped him. A silence fell between them. It carried the pair down the road and into the complex where they were waved in thanks to the Witness. He stood just inside the fenced area next to a bruised and battered soldier. The wounded man struggled to finish his cigarette, his hands shaking before him.

"My friend here was relaying what happened." The Witness offered the man a sympathetic smile. "Go ahead."

The cigarette shook between his fingers; ash dusted the soldier's pants. Bloodshot eyes stared through them, lost to memory. "She wasn't human. The way she moved? Couldn't be. And I clipped her. I know I did. It was right in the leg. Didn't stop her. Didn't even faze her."

"You shot her?" Metcalf asked.

"I did," he said. "But when I went to look, there was no blood. Not a damn drop."

Metcalf peered at the Witness, who offered a silent nod of confirmation. It must have been part of the transformation. He had mentioned increased strength, but there were more side effects that none of them realized.

"Why here?" She peered around the complex. The buildings appeared innocuous enough, yet with the presence of so many armed guards, there was more to the place than it seemed. "Why would she come to this facility?"

"Signet is a cover," the soldier answered. He kept his voice low, unable to make eye contact — not even with his fellow officers. "We house evidence lockers, access codes, and research data for a dozen different departments. Never had a break-in. Heck, this detail is pretty boring, to tell you the truth. Before today, at any rate."

"What was taken?" Metcalf said with growing concern.

"I..." The young man stopped and shook his head. "I can't. My superiors will—"

The Witness' hand fell on the soldier's shoulder. "They will want to know you're doing everything you can to rectify this tragedy."

The soldier caught his reflection in the man's glasses. He sucked in the snot hanging from his nostrils, then spit a wad of phlegm onto the pavement. Standing, the young man tried to clean himself up. He tossed the cigarette to the ground and stamped it out.

He cleared his throat, yet the words remained quiet against the whipping wind. "Data. All related to a virus being studied by the CDC."

"What kind of—"

"That's all?" the Witness asked over Metcalf. She wanted more information, anything that might identify a possible viral agent at play in this situation. The Witness, however, shook his head. Whatever it was didn't matter to his agenda, and she wondered if their paths lined up as neatly as she had once believed.

"No," the soldier replied. "She took ID tags, access codes, and a transport from the lot."

"A transport?" Kanigher chimed in. "Why?"

"No idea," the young man said with a shrug. "It's only meant for pickups and deliveries to Memphis International." The second he mentioned the name of the local airport, his eyes widened in terror. He scrambled for his radio. "Oh, God. Did we call it in?"

The other soldiers near him said nothing.

"Hey!" he yelled to them. "Anyone call in the transport?"

No one offered a confirmation. The soldier pulled his radio free. He moved for the gate. "I'm sorry. I have to—"

"Understood," the Witness said with a tip of his hat. "We'll do what we can on our end."

Kanigher cocked an eyebrow. "Really?"

"We should assist if we can, shouldn't we, Bobby?"

The name held in the air. Metcalf's pet name for her friend uttered by the Witness caused Kanigher's teeth to grind. "Cute," he uttered. "What do we do now?"

Already in motion, Metcalf tapped the comm in her ear. "Riley? You need to get to the airport. Quick as you can."

# CHAPTER TEN

Sitting down for a meal was no longer an option for Zac. Any chance he had to have a decent rest after the blur of the last few days vanished the moment he noticed the men and women tailing his position.

The sedan at the side of the road made its way into the lot. Cruising casually, it took a spot far enough away to appear inconspicuous, yet with a clear sight line of the front door. The two so-called joggers at the end of the building made their intentions to head inside known with boisterous laughter, which rang false.

The more time Zac spent tinkering with his keys, the more people he realized were out of place in the area. A van was stationed across the street in the loading zone of a closed storefront. Flashes of light reflected the sun down on the lot. When Zac glanced up, he noted three men along the rooftop of a jewelry store. They were dressed as maintenance workers but carried few tools between them.

The IHOP might have provided Zac a moment to catch his breath, but it also trapped him. He needed space, but getting back into the car would have immediately signaled his intent to his watchers. Instead, Zac pulled at the handle of the door once more to ensure it was locked, then started down the sidewalk. He passed the pair of joggers at the door. One held the door for him to enter.

Zac nodded to them with a false smile. "I'm good. Thanks."

He continued down the walkway and through the parking lot. He passed the sedan with the tinted windows. The moment it was behind him, Zac's pace quickened for the McDonald's next door, and he stepped inside.

Getting in line, Zac tried his best to slow his pulse and ease his mind. The voice in the back of his head screamed for escape. April was smart enough to see his dilemma with that plan: there was no way for Zac to know just how many people were involved in this operation, and no way to slip away from them all because of that open question.

Three people stood in front of him. Grateful for the reprieve to plan his next move, Zac let out a long breath. Subtle shifts allowed him to look out the windows that surrounded the fast-food joint. The van remained across the street, while the sedan shifted from the neighboring lot to face the new eatery. The maintenance workers were no longer on the roof, but down on the street—no tools to be seen still.

When the joggers started for McDonald's, Zac realized the clock was ticking down for him. He didn't know where to go, or what to do, to escape his followers. He didn't even know who they were, or what they could want with him. April's instincts, however, took over: running was the only option left for him.

"Where?" he whispered. A stray glance flew his way from the woman in front of him. He simply smiled and ducked away from her. Shifting out of line, Zac leaned on the recently cleaned counter. "Any thoughts?"

"You sure you want an answer?" April asked in his mind. Her visage shimmered on the counter. "It might hurt."

The joggers at the door took their time to enter. The effort was for his benefit, so as not to spook him, though they needn't have bothered: Zac was plenty spooked. "Do it."

Images flooded Zac's head. He gripped the side of the counter tight; pain threatened to send him to the floor. A scream built up in his lungs, but he swallowed it down. He did the same with the flood of information filling his subconscious mind. The Wellspring programming showed him the city of Grand Island. From a topographical map to a street-by-street layout, Zac discovered every entry point and exit to the place.

Jangling bells welcomed the joggers to the restaurant. They also shook Zac back to reality. He saw everything so clearly. Biting back the residual pain from the intense download, Zac pushed away from the counter. He started for the exit on the far side. Looking over his shoulder was his only mistake. The second the joggers made eye contact with him, they knew they had been made.

"He's bolting!" one exclaimed into their radio, tied neatly to their wrist.

"Get him!" the other yelled. She broke into a run, but Zac was already in the lot doing the same.

Everyone converged on him. The maintenance workers pulled out Tasers, the only tools they needed for the job at hand. The sedan's tires squealed as it hopped the curb to block Zac's escape.

Zac followed all their movements, then raced deeper into the lot. A dumpster sat in front of a ten-foot fence. Climbing atop the disgusting refuse dump, Zac pulled himself over the fence and into the neighboring alley.

Over the pounding of his heart, Zac noted the frantic cries from the surveillance team. A sly smirk broke across his lips. He let that feeling carry him down the alley and out into the neighboring street.

Traffic roared. Construction tied up much of the area. In the back of his mind, Zac realized it was related to a blown pipe due to age and the crumbling infrastructure. The knowledge came easier and with less pain, though he tried not to wonder what he had lost in the exchange.

He needed the edge.

The van rounded the corner, powering through the cars on the road. Horns blared from angry commuters late for appointments or just pissed off about spending unnecessary time stuck in traffic. Zac cut across the street. He worked through the maze of slow-moving cars at a steady clip. The van fared far worse. They tried to push their way through, but struggled to penetrate an unyielding wall of vehicles at the end of the block. Eventually, they surrendered to the traffic. Two men vacated the van and started for Zac's position.

Zac, however, had turned the corner. He ran along the sidewalk and through the meandering crowds of daytime shoppers in the district. Apologies were offered in tandem with more collisions until he spotted an elderly gentleman vacating his apartment building. Zac leaped over the side of the stoop, then climbed the stairs two at a time. As the old man let go of the door, Zac caught it in his hand and slipped inside.

Pulling it shut secured the lock. Zac fell back a step, his chest heaving from exertion. He dabbed at his forehead to mop up a puddle of sweat, then turned for the stairs. The climb up the towering four stories was long, but he couldn't take the chance of a resident reporting him for trespassing.

Zac nearly cheered when he pushed the door open to the roof and faced the sunshine. Not only had he given himself the distance he needed, but the roof allowed him a view of the entire street. He kept low as he reached the ledge. The men from the van raced past the building without a glance up. The joggers did the same from across the street.

Zac settled along the ledge to cool down and calm his nerves. The peace lasted only a moment before a voice called out from the other side of the roof.

"No more running, Zac."

The voice slammed into his memory worse than anything the Wellspring had shared over their time together. The second the figure came into view, Zac placed the voice—one he hadn't heard in months.

"Henry?" Zac asked.

Henry Reed wore a red hooded sweatshirt and faded blue jeans. His shoelaces were untied and hung down the sides of his heavily worn sneakers. Zac's focus, however, remained on the young man's hands. Flames danced along Henry's fingertips and hovered over his palms in deep oranges and reds.

"Not another step, Zac," he said, the fire caught in his eyes. "You're coming with me."

# CHAPTER ELEVEN

The transport ambled into the turn. The small inlet was well-hidden among the fenced-off portion of the tarmac that made up the Memphis International Airport, but the sunshine gave a clear view of where Juniper needed to go.

A slight detour to collect her cargo allowed her the chance to wipe away the blood that stained her skin and clean out the flesh that stuck beneath her fingernails and in her hair. She wore it all like a badge of honor during the fight, but none suited her for her present task.

With an ID pinned to her chest, the army fatigues on full display, Juniper idled up to the waiting gate. The arm continued to block her path, forcing the stolen transport to stop. A guard inside the station house glanced up from his monitor, then back down again. He raised a finger to give him a moment. Another guard stepped forward, an arrogant smirk on his lips at the sight of Juniper behind the wheel.

"ID please."

"Sure thing," she said in an amused tone at his obvious interest.

He took the badge in hand, letting it rest on his clipboard. He marked down the name BRITTANY CHAMBERS—she had committed the name to memory on the way over—and set about circling the jeep. "Call came in only a minute or two ago. Cutting it close with the notification today."

"Miscommunication," she answered. She stuck her head out the window for him to hear her better, but also to keep an eye on his search. He opened the back of the transport where two crates were strapped down for travel. When he closed the hatch again, she offered him a grateful smile. "You know how it is."

"No kidding."

Every time he flashed his teeth at her, Juniper imagined ripping them from his face. Every time she blinked, an image of the man's beaten and broken body sent waves of pleasure through her. Roleplaying was a waste of time in her view. Violence made things much easier, and so much more satisfying. Still, she did her best, given her instructions and the precious cargo in the back.

"Gotta love bureaucracy."

The guard nodded. "Just give us a minute."

"Will do."

She tried to maintain her composure, tried to imagine what Brittany Chambers would say or think, having to stomach the leering eyes of these so-called men to get through a simple task like an airport drop-off. It sickened Juniper right to her core.

As she waited, she wondered what sound the guard's neck would make as it snapped under her fingers. She pictured how many bones might shatter under her blows before he fell in a fight. If it was anything like the fools back at the Signet facility, it would not take much effort on her part.

The world was weak. People struggled for dominance through the use of words rather than strength. She knew better. In this new life, Juniper saw things much more clearly. Nothing could stand in her way: not these two guards, not the men and women back at Signet — no one.

"Everything okay?" Juniper called from the transport.

The guards continued to work within the station house. At the sound of her call, the one with the devilish grin returned.

"One second," he said. "Computers take time."

He shifted closer to the jeep. He rested his arm on the open window ledge. Juniper inched deeper into the vehicle for space, and to hold back the urge to snap the man in two for his arrogance.

The guard looked back at his partner. "We clear?" No answer came. The guard sidled up to the transport, his head nearly inside the cabin. "I'm sure it's fine. First time on the delivery run?"

"How could you tell?" Juniper tried to maintain the conversation, as well as her flowery attitude. Her hands gripped the wheel tighter, and her eyes strained ahead rather than meet the guard's soulful gaze. It was all she could do to avoid exacting an unholy terror on the station house and the personnel within.

A hand rose within the station. The guard pulled away from the transport. He headed inside for another discussion.

The second he left, Juniper let out a long breath. She maintained her grip on the steering wheel, the sharpness of her nails ripping the cover.

The guard returned seconds later. He held out a pass. "Here you go."

"Thanks." Juniper took the pass in hand, then tossed it along the dash.

The gate lifted before her. Slowly, she crept the transport forward, more than ready to move on with her mission before she did something the master would find most regrettable. That was the last thing she wanted.

Seconds after passing the gate, the guard's voice rang out. "Hold up!"

Tires squealed as the brakes took hold. Juniper peered out her window, curious. "Yes?"

Another slip of paper tore from the man's clipboard, and he held it out for her. "You forgot your hangar number."

"Right," she said with a laugh. She accepted the paper. "Crazy day."

"Tell me about it." He leaned on the side of the transport once more. "You're heading to 14-F. Think you can find it or do you need me to —"

"I can find it," Juniper said quickly.

Ego deflated, the guard retreated from the transport. "Oh. Okay. Good."

"14-F," she repeated. He nodded in agreement. "Perfect. Thank you."

She hit the accelerator and left the station behind. The slip number remained in her grip. Looking it over once more, Juniper tossed it aside. Other arrangements had already been made for her.

Passing multiple depots and skirting around other attendants working hard to keep the airport intact, Juniper found her way to the far side of the field. A small jetliner waited in an open hangar bay.

Juniper backed the transport inside. She came to a halt near the back of the plane where the cargo hold was opened and ready to receive her goods. Stepping out of the vehicle, Juniper set to work unloading the crates. Their weight was no issue for her and they easily found their way inside the back of the plane.

A shadow loomed behind her as she finished. "You have everything we need?"

A genuine smile filled her face. Just the sound of the master's voice was enough to calm her violent tendencies — at least for a little while.

"Yes."

Juniper moved for the jeep. The passenger-side door opened, and she removed a small case with the stolen items from Signet. Her master took the case in hand. His other rubbed the outer shell as if it held a grand prize within.

"Excellent work, my dear," he said. "Excellent work."

# CHAPTER TWELVE

Morgan's hands strangled the steering wheel. Tension clearly ran through her body, her teeth grinding against each other at the slightest noise. And there sure as hell was plenty of noise around her.

It was Ben's fault. His reading of the directions was unnecessary, the phone more than capable of handling their course from Millington for the airport. Ever since the end of their last conversation, however, Ben had tried to insert himself wherever he could to get her talking again.

Whenever they fell silent with each other, trouble followed. It was a recurring theme, and one he refused to stick with during the current mission. He had been wrong to hold back what he'd learned about Metcalf and the Witness, but he couldn't let that split their focus. For once, he recognized the priority and fought to keep them on the path—even if the very sound of his voice sparked fury in his partner's eyes.

Her lack of familiarity with Memphis didn't help. Midday traffic clustered throughout the downtown area, which forced her to cut a swath around the highways and down back roads to circumvent any delays.

"Take a left at the next intersection," Ben said.

She nodded, though he swore sparks flew from between her teeth. His withholding of intel hurt her, and he cursed his reticence to share.

The simple truth was Ben didn't know what to make of the information. Talking with the Witness about it brought no clarity on the subject, either. Ben knew Morgan deserved to hear the truth, to bring some sense to the subject. Now, however, Ben was too late to initiate the conversation, and he paid the price for his silence.

Behind them, Nixon and Adler worked diligently. They tapped away at their separate stations. Out of everyone in the department, they proved to be the most professional.

"The airport is four miles away," Nixon announced. Ben lifted the phone so his companion could see the distance displayed, relaying the same information. Nixon shot him a dubious glare and pointed to his screen. "We're not going to want the main entrance."

"Then where?" Ben asked.

"If we circle east from the parking area, there is a security gate."

Ben widened the view on the screen. He couldn't see it; the app was not anywhere close to being as handy as the man in the back of the van. Ben passed the phone over. Nixon looked over the current route. His finger fell on Louis Carruthers Drive, and the small opening to indicate the gate in question.

"There." He tossed the device back to Ben.

"Thanks."

Adler shifted her seat closer. "I'm working on a cover story."

"Morgan, take the left!"

The wheel turned sharply. The van slipped between two oncoming cars. It barely scrapped past the second to clear the turn. Horns blared and angry shouts followed them as they continued on their way.

Their screams filled the cabin as a tractor-trailer came into view. It backed into a parking lot slowly. The van jerked to the right to avoid the front end of the vehicle, its tires bumping against the curb.

"Morgan, you need to—"

"The gate should be—"

"If we tell them—"

"Guys!" Morgan shouted after traffic calmed down. "Enough with the yelling and the talking over each other. For one whole minute, I don't want to hear a word. From any of you."

"But—"

Morgan stopped Ben, who continued to hold out his phone. She snatched it from him and set it on the dash.

"The GPS is fully capable of directing me where I want to

go."

"Morgan..."

"One. Minute," she snapped.

The cabin fell silent. Morgan let out a deep breath. She settled into her seat. All eyes remained on her. Even the tapping of the keyboards quieted to help.

Ben, of course, found the silence irritating. His foot tapped along the floor, and his hands ran along his pants until he couldn't hold the words in any longer.

"Morgan?" he asked.

Angry eyes spun to greet him. "What?"

"You went through a red light back there," Ben said in a quiet voice. "Just saying."

Morgan groaned with clear frustration. "Please let me shoot something, or God help him."

"I can hear you."

"I'm aware," she replied.

Reaching the outskirts of the airport's footprint, Morgan circled the terminal. Nixon's directions were on point, and they found their way along the side of the tarmac until they caught sight of the small opening in the chain-link fence for entry.

"The gate is—"

Morgan raised a hand to stop Nixon. "I see it."

"It's..." he muttered. "It's right ahead, is all."

The gate came up quickly. Only a single vehicle was ahead of them, and Morgan eased the van behind it. She turned to Ben, clearly waiting for a comment about their drive and the many traffic violations committed along the journey.

Ben mimicked a lock along his lips. Morgan rolled her eyes at the juvenile act, then leaned over the center console for the back of the van, and the silent member of their team.

"Adler?"

Adler hesitated until Morgan offered a nod of approval to speak up. She leaned in close. "I used Signet's call signature. You're clear to enter."

The vehicle ahead of them entered the field. Two guards waved them forward to the lowering gate.

Morgan smiled. "See? Someone can be useful around here."

Ben huffed. "I can be useful."

"Yet you choose not to be," Morgan shot back. "Why is that?"

Ben shrugged. "More fun?"

Morgan held her tongue, a forced smile on her face to greet the guards. Ben ignored the back and forth, including the flirtatious vibe from one of the men in uniform. Morgan played it off masterfully, but Ben wanted none of it. He scouted ahead, noting the massive amount of commercial traffic surrounding the airport.

They were moving before Ben realized the conversation had ended at the gate.

"Get his number?" She passed the sheet of paper over to him. "What's 14-F?"

"Hangar number." She threw him a satisfied smirk. "His number's on the back."

"Lucky," he chided.

She ripped the paper from him and let it fall to the ground. "Keep an eye out."

"You just passed the hangar."

Morgan nodded. "No transport. So where could they—"

Ben pointed ahead. "There."

The front of the stolen jeep stuck out of the bay. The Signet logo was clear along the passenger door. "Found it. Useful enough?"

The van halted in front of the bay. No one was present, and the transport had been emptied.

"Now where?"

Adler shot forward. "That plane."

"How do you—"

"The manifest shows it was stationed here," she said. Nixon lifted his laptop for them to view, but no one bothered. The plane was prepping for departure.

"Look," Ben said. Two figures stood outside the plane. One pointed in their direction, and the second tracked his movement. She started for the position of their van as the first took to the stairs of the plane. "What does she think she's doing?"

"Doesn't matter." Morgan slammed on the gas to meet their opponent head-on. "She's given us an opening and we're taking it."

The plane was almost a mile down the runway. The woman, however, barreled toward them. Distance obviously meant nothing to her. Her legs pumped in tune with her arms. Each stride carried her closer until her legs bent low and she jumped into the air.

"Whoa," Ben exclaimed. He leaned along the dash for a better view out of the windshield. The silhouette of the woman was lost in the sunlight. "Where did she—"

The woman dropped out of the sky like a blazing comet. She crashed on the hood of the van, a maniacal grin on her face.

"What the hell?" The van screeched from the impact. The engine smoked, and their speed lagged. Gripping tight to the hood with her left hand, the woman's right hand pulled back, fist clenched, then shot forward. The windshield splintered, obscuring their view.

"Morgan—"

"Shoot her already!" the frantic driver yelled.

Ben pulled out his sidearm. He aimed, yet hesitated. He couldn't take the chance of a ricochet hitting Morgan. "I can't."

"Fine," Morgan said, seething with anger. She slammed on the brake. The van squealed to a halt.

Their attacker lost her grip. Flying backward, her body skipped along the tarmac like a stone on the water. She came to rest in a heap. Steam rose from her arms and legs.

Ben undid his belt and opened the door. Morgan rounded the van, her sidearm at the ready. Ben held her back for a second with a curious gaze. "Did she look familiar to you?"

Morgan shook her head. Hurried steps carried them from the van to the woman who remained curled up on the side of the runway.

"I swear I've seen her before," Ben said.

Morgan moved for the body, waving him back a step. "Cover me."

"Don't, Morgan," Ben said. "I think it's a bad idea."

Morgan ignored him. The woman was crazy enough to attack them, yet Morgan would have moved heaven and earth to keep her breathing. That was the doctor in her, something innate to Morgan's thinking.

Morgan reached for the body. She took her by the arm and pushed the wounded warrior over for a better view. At the sight of the woman's face, Morgan staggered back a step. Her hand moved to her lips, and her eyes sparked with recognition.

"You... you're right, Ben," Morgan said. "I have seen her before. I—"

The woman's eyes flew open. She shot up on her feet before Morgan. Her arm swung in a wide arc and caught Morgan on her left side. Morgan's Glock flew from her hand; her body soared ten feet in the air before slamming back to the ground with a hard thud.

"Morgan!" Ben opened fire. The woman took three shots to the chest but never faltered. Her smile grew with each impact. "Holy shit."

Ben leveled the gun at her once again. This time, however, she didn't bother to wait. She turned and leaped toward the waiting plane. Her body lifted twenty feet into the air and landed just short of the steps.

Morgan's groan woke Ben to his injured partner. "Hey," he called as he raced to her side. She held out a hand. Taking it, Ben helped her to her feet, though she maintained a tight grip on her side. "You okay?"

He knew better. Nevertheless, she nodded. "Bellbrook," she said. "That woman was from Bellbrook."

Ben remembered her vividly. She had been the store clerk, the one who had cut Ruth Heller while they had been trying to help her. Ben recalled the woman being much heavier and older in appearance.

"June," he said, recalling the woman's name. "When did she turn into a badass?"

"The chrysalis," Morgan said. "But who—"

Both looked to the tarmac and the waiting plane. June waved from the base of the steps before joining her companion at the top. The gentleman ushered her aboard. His cold eyes, so penetrating even from afar, stared down the pair of shocked agents.

His very presence halted their pursuit. Not that it would have mattered. The second the man stepped inside, the plane barreled into position for takeoff. There was no way to catch up once it started. The image of the man haunted them: a man they had seen multiple times in the past, and who always brought with him nothing but pain and misery.

"Howard Clevinger," Ben said. "You've got to be kidding me."

"We need to get to the van." Morgan winced in pain with each step. "We need to contact Metcalf, and—"

"Morgan," Ben stopped her. "We might have bigger problems."

Sirens blared. Airport security raced toward their position from both ends of the tarmac. The flashing lights and screams for surrender echoed in the air. Ben and Morgan slowly raised their hands over their heads.

Catching Clevinger would have to wait.

# CHAPTER THIRTEEN

Twin bursts of flame shot out at Zac. He dove to avoid the full brunt of the blasts. The heat seared his back, and he scampered across the roof. Fire trailed behind him. An air conditioning unit caught the brunt as Zac ducked behind it for cover. The unit sizzled and fried from the heat. The electrical conduit to the building sparked until the entire apparatus failed and fell silent.

Zac crept away from the scalding unit. He remained tucked behind obstacles, trying to get out of the line of fire. It was a poor choice of words, considering his attacker.

The thought of Henry Reed made Zac want to scream. Henry had been caught in the middle of a murder investigation in Chicago. His flame powers had sparked at the absolute wrong time and ended up taking a life that would have ended his own had he not acted. During the case, Zac had found himself at the mercy of the young man, and while frightened at first, the two had bonded. When all had been said and done, they had left the Windy City as friends.

The notion of friendship caused Zac to stop running. He raised his hands, then shifted out into plain view. "Henry!" he called. "It's me. You don't have to do this."

Henry's sad eyes glowed. Flames danced in his irises. "I do, though," he said. Fire consumed the young man's hands, though it tapered enough to see his skin in the center of the flames. "I'm sorry, Zac. This is my only way out."

Heat rose from the man's chest. The air wavered along the rooftop. Zac felt the rising temperature surround him. Henry was building up steam for a fresh attack.

Zac turned for the edge of the roof. His back continued to irritate him from the initial strike, and he could tell his clothes had been scorched during the affair. It didn't deter him or give him pause, though. He ran for his life.

"This is your fault, Zac!" Henry shouted after him.

Zac leaped from the roof to the neighboring building. He moved for the door to head back down to the street. It was locked. Henry closed the distance quickly.

"You sent me to them," Henry said. A fireball erupted from his fingertips. It collided with the doorway. Metal fused and melted. Henry had never displayed that level of control before, not even at the hospital in Chicago, where he had ended the lives of a mercenary team sent to dispatch everyone connected with Project Promethean.

Something had changed in Henry. Something had triggered a deeper understanding of his innate talent. Frightened by the young man's power, Zac left the fused door for the edge of the next roof.

"Do you know what they did to me? The tests? The pain?"

Zac turned at the questions. He regretted it immediately. Twisting to face Henry, his feet slipped on the gravelly roof. He fell to the ground with a crash. Stone scrapped his cheek upon impact.

It was a lucky thing, too. Another pair of fireballs skirted the sky above him mere seconds after his tumble. The hair on Zac's head started to singe at their proximity. Henry wasn't playing around.

Zac jumped to his feet. "I thought you were safe, Henry. I thought we had saved you."

Henry's entire body lit up like a pyre. "They tortured me! They forced me to use my powers for them. Just like they did to my mother!"

"I... I didn't know."

The words felt hollow. Ignorance never justified failure. He had thought Henry to be safe at a DSA facility in Florida: a place named the Ark. It had been commissioned to help people like Henry, those who had been twisted genetically either through sheer miracle or by some coordinated effort. The Ark had been set up to help train special people in their talents, and safeguard them from being taken advantage of out in the world.

Or so Zac had been led to believe. Instead, Henry ended up

being manipulated just as his mother had been before her death. She had been a Trust asset for years. Her task had always been the same: take out the target—to kill, without knowing the why of any of it.

Zac hadn't known the truth about the Ark, not until Greg Sullivan had made it clear after his coup. The cases handled by the DSA had fed right into the Trust's interests. They were the true masterminds behind everything and controlled the board from start to finish.

"I made a deal," Henry said. His body cooled until only a glimmer of flame remained on his hand. "They made the offer, and I took it, not that I had a choice in the matter."

"Henry…"

"I can get my freedom, Zac," Henry continued. "All they want is you."

Zac's feet slid along the rooftop. They caught the ledge, and he nearly tumbled over. Catching himself with his hands, Zac noticed the wide gap between buildings. There was nowhere left to run.

Henry blocked all other avenues of escape.

"They won't follow through, Henry," Zac said. "They're still using you. Can't you see that?"

"I have to try," Henry replied. He slowly approached. With each step, Zac's chances evaporated. Yet, he failed to move, failed to do anything other than wallow in his past mistake. "Give yourself up. They want the Wellspring, and you're going to tell them everything you know about it."

*What I know about it?* Zac almost laughed at the phrasing. They still hadn't figured out what happened at the Cove. The Trust needed the Wellspring back, secure in one of their facilities for further study and control.

Zac was now that Wellspring. He refused to play the puppet for them or anyone. Escape was the only option left to him.

"I won't," Zac said. He started for Henry. "I won't help them. I won't tell them anything. I'm sorry for what happened to you, Henry. I truly am."

"Zac," Henry pleaded. His arm reached for the man he had once called friend. He recalled every ounce of flame. With it gone, Henry looked just as he had all those months ago in Chicago: young and innocent. "Please come with me."

"I can't," Zac said. "I'm sorry."

Zac spun on his heels. He dug down, then launched for the edge of the roof. The neighboring building was at least ten feet away, but he had to make it. There was too much for him to do still. The signal needed to be stopped. He needed to see his wife and son again, to rebuild their lives together.

"ZAC!" Henry bellowed.

Zac stepped on the ledge. His momentum carried him forward and pushed him into his leap for the next building. Beneath him, Zac felt the ground give way.

For a moment, Zac believed he would make it, that he could elude the torture of the Wellspring. He could beat his fate. The roof was inches before him; his fingers stretched to take hold.

Then the fall began.

Gravity beckoned and pulled him down. The brick of the adjacent building blurred as the speed of his descent picked up. Zac fell, a scream on his lips the entire way. Hands flailing, like a bird trying to flap its wings, Zac reached for anything to help — anything that might save his worthless, little life.

Two floors from the ground, Zac snatched a cable line hanging between buildings. He held tight, hoping the line would support his weight. For a single second it did, then it snapped free at one end. Zac's body swung in a shallow arc and he slammed into the side of the adjacent building. Still carrying too much momentum, he bounded off the brick. The cable slipped from his grasp.

The fall continued.

Staring up toward the roof, Zac caught one last glimpse of Henry. The young man's eyes trailed him into the deep darkness of the alley. No hate resided in them any longer, no rage at their shared past, only terror of what came next.

With that fear rooted in his heart, Zac closed his eyes and hit the ground.

# CHAPTER FOURTEEN

They had lost hours at the airport. As the minutes passed, Morgan's anger over the entire affair grew. The same questions circled them. They had been thrown together, then separated, and finally reunited in a never-ending parade of ignorance displayed by the authorities at the Memphis International Airport.

The blame didn't rest with local law enforcement. No, the fault lay with the field team. If the DSA had still been around in an official capacity, had they still been working within government channels, none of this would have happened.

By the time Metcalf had arrived, the afternoon had vanished. Morgan, Ben, and the others had been released — assurances made thanks to their false credentials. Rather than depart the terminal completely, they loitered outside the row of eateries in Terminal B.

All six of them sat around a large table. Nixon and Adler kept their heads down, quietly resting. Metcalf and Kanigher grumbled between each other to plan out their next moves. Only the Witness remained standing. He circled the entire area, offering nods and well wishes to the authorities, who continued to monitor the team from a distance.

Morgan tried to catch her breath. Her side ached from June's blow. The on-site medic did her best to patch Morgan up, and the gauze wrapped tight around her mid-section certainly improved her demeanor. Still, her side hurt.

Beside her, Ben sipped loudly at his drink. Each strained ingestion from his straw made her want to scream. Morgan tried to focus on something else, anything else, but when she viewed the cold sandwich before her and the looks of defeat from her colleagues, she found herself too overwhelmed to remain quiet any longer.

"This isn't embarrassing at all."

"It's not so bad." Ben sucked harder on his straw. "Did you know this airport has a smoothie stand?"

Morgan's eyes thinned. "Seriously?"

Ben nodded. "I'm getting another before we leave."

"If we leave," Morgan muttered. She glanced around at the added security thanks to their presence. "We're more likely to be tossed in a cell and left to rot."

The Witness stopped his pacing and leaned between them. "We're free to leave at any time, Agent Dunleavy. I've patched things up with security."

"See?" Ben said. "Don't you feel better now? Glasses vouched for us."

"Oh, I'm sure," Morgan said with quiet disdain.

"You're welcome." The Witness patted Ben's shoulder, then returned to his pacing. Ben let go of the smoothie and shifted along his stool.

"No one's thanking you, Glasses," Ben called to the man. "You put us in this situation."

It was true enough, but didn't tell the entire story. While the Witness pulled them into the affair, the blame for the theft at the lumber mill belonged to someone else. It was someone none of them expected, but could no longer deny after watching him fly off into the sunset like a damn cowboy at the end of an old Western flick.

"No." Morgan locked eyes with Ben and held his full attention. "*He* did."

Ben slowly nodded. "Clevinger."

The name pulled everyone back to the conversation. It stirred Nixon and Adler from their rest and ended the grumbling of the others.

Metcalf cleared her throat. Her hands clasped before her on the edge of the table. "Care to share with the class, Morgan?"

They all knew the name to some extent. The Clevinger name had followed the DSA ever since Bellbrook, when they'd found Howard in the back of an electronics store. He had been trying to stave off the effects of the signal unleashed by the Witness. The field team's untimely intervention had upended the man's plans for self-preservation.

Caught in the throes of the virus, Clevinger had assaulted Morgan. When she closed her eyes, she could still see the bullets ripping through his chest. His life had ended in pain and misery, but the name had continued to plague Morgan even after his death.

There had been another Howard Clevinger in Buffalo. In fact, three more had been discovered in pursuit of their wayward brother. Each had had their own agenda. Each had been playing their own game with the lives of those around them.

"He's a clone," she said with a clear voice. The team leaned closer to keep their volume down, and not draw any more ire from the security personnel monitoring their behavior. "Howard Clevinger, the real one—if he still exists—created clones of himself to help with his research. Guess how it turned out?"

The Witness nodded. "I stole his work in Bellbrook. I was not aware of other iterations, but now it makes sense."

"What does?" Ben remarked.

"Someone else was tracking the project or the man," the Witness explained. "I never figured out which. Now I know it must have been another Clevinger."

"Not just any other," Morgan said. "Not with what we've learned of the clones."

"Morgan?" Ben asked, confused.

"He wanted something specific at Signet."

"Details relating to a virus," Metcalf confirmed with a nod. She stared intently at the Witness, who did his best to ignore the remark. "As well as CDC ID tags."

"Right," Morgan said. "A virus? The CDC? Perverting the Witness' precious Bellbrook experiment? Ben, you saw June tonight."

"She was fierce," Ben said, following her train of thought. "Vicious, and loving every second of it."

"Angry, yet focused."

Recognition filled his face. "Oh, hell. You're saying—"

"The CDC doesn't study happy viruses, and this man thrives on destruction." Morgan fought to slow her spinning thoughts. Everything made sense to her now. "He lives for pure chaos. We barely survived him in Buffalo, but this? This is next level for him."

Ben ran his hand through his hair. He clearly tried to find another rationale. The effort failed quickly. "You're right. It has to be him."

The others waited for more, patient to give Morgan the time she needed. "When Clevinger attempted to wipe away the mistakes of the past to build the perfect lab assistant, he ended up creating his own worst nightmare. One willing to kill millions to get revenge on his creator."

He had already taken the lives of three of his so-called brothers. Hunting them down like prey, he had wiped them from existence to erase his "father's" work.

He was no longer Howard Clevinger, not in the strictest sense of the word. No, this clone was something more now.

Morgan met each of their eyes. "He calls himself Thirteen."

# CHAPTER FIFTEEN

"Items on the belt," the officer said. "Step through the scanner."

The man's tone was robotic, the instructions obviously ordered every minute of every day while on shift. Still, the head of a group of four warmly welcomed the officers with an enthusiastic wave.

Fort Collins might not have been the prestigious home for the main office of the Centers for Disease Control, but the satellite hub was impressive in scale. The building towered over twenty-stories, the largest structure in the area by far. It was separated from much of the downtown area, fenced off and gated to keep the general public out, as well as surrounded by roads that offered no entry anywhere near the place.

The entire facility was isolated to hide the dangerous work held within. There were secrets hidden on each level, viral agents that might wipe out entire city blocks in an instant if any of the protective measures failed to hold.

Apocalyptic dreams danced behind the eyes of Thirteen the moment he stepped through the welcoming scanner. For him, the visit was the equivalent of finding the North Pole and being greeted by Santa Claus himself.

"Incredible," he muttered.

"All clear." The officer nodded toward Thirteen's waiting briefcase.

Thirteen collected his gear. "Thank you, sir. You have a wonderful day."

The officer cracked a smile. It took some effort. "You too, Doc."

"Oh, I know I will." Thirteen straightened at the appellation. He needled the tag clipped to his lapel, a gift from the Signet facility.

Juniper followed close, two more of her brethren at her backside. They all wore suits, but continued to stretch and pull at the fabric. Being tucked inside crates so they could be stowed away on their plane had taken a toll on them, but they acclimated quickly to their newfound freedom. The move was necessary to make the trip with the least amount of questions asked, as well as to avoid security at Memphis International. They lacked any form of identity beyond the name caught on their lips at their rebirth. Everything else came from Thirteen, and he merely required their compliance, not their comfort.

Thirteen kept a close eye on his companions. With each interaction, there was a flash of violence tucked in their eyes. Juniper was the worst of the trio, the two men at her back better able to control the rage programmed into them. It was a late addition, one of the triumphs Thirteen claimed during his studies after locating the lumber mill.

The signal virus had changed them, reduced their intelligence level to infants. The task had been put on Thirteen to bring them back up to speed. He had done so the only way he knew how: through manipulation and chemicals. The Bellbrook Batch was his pride and joy, and only the beginning of the trials to come.

"I wasn't aware of any visitors today," a voice called from the elevator banks. He stood over six-feet tall, his gut helping him fill a good chunk of the corridor. A thin white beard blanketed his cheeks. Beady eyes greeted Thirteen and his cohort. "I'm Richard Thompson, head of this office."

"A pleasure." Thirteen took the man's hand from his side and shook it without prompting. "You have done an absolutely marvelous job here."

"Thank you…"

"Oh." Thirteen let go of the man's hand. He ushered his companions forward. "These are my colleagues. Juniper, Kenneth, and William."

"I'm sorry," Richard said. He shook his head, confused. "That doesn't explain anything. Who are you, and what are you doing in my building?"

"Important work, my friend." Thirteen punched the call button for the elevator. The doors immediately opened on the car at their side. "Some might say the will of God Himself, but I don't like to brag."

"What?" Richard asked. Juniper's hand fell on his shoulder and guided the stupefied director into the elevator. "Where are you taking me?"

"Somewhere we can talk," Thirteen said. He turned toward Kenneth and William. "You two know what to do?"

"Yes, sir," Kenneth said. His chest swelled against the suit, his body bristling with muscle.

"Make sure we are not disturbed and then proceed to your objective." Thirteen passed along his briefcase to Kenneth, then entered the car. The doors slid to a close the moment he crossed the threshold.

"What objective?" Richard called out. "I demand to know what the hell you are doing here this instant, and where you received these entry badges!"

The doors shut with a clang. Thirteen smiled. "From the Signet facility."

Richard's eyes widened. "You..." He spun to face Juniper. "You were the one who—"

Juniper nodded. Her hands shot up and clamped down on the sides of Richard's head. Squeezing ever so lightly, the woman's smile grew at the sound of her victim's scream.

"Oh, hush now," Thirteen said. Juniper eased her pressure, twisting around so her master could face their escort. "Tell me what I need to know, and you'll survive this brief altercation."

"Never," Richard said. "Security will stop you. They will—"

"Be dead in a matter of minutes," Thirteen replied. "You see, my briefcase wasn't as clean as your scanners assumed. A deadly agent has been filling the lobby since my arrival. Rather nasty way to go. You'll be glad we managed to sneak away in time."

"You... you're insane!"

"Practical," Thirteen responded. "Our time is limited, and I intend to make it count. Now, the storage lab. Which floor?"

"I won't—"

Thirteen sighed and backed away. "Juniper?"

The squeezing returned. Pressure mounted from both sides, the sound of popping and cracking growing against the man's skull.

With a wave, Thirteen ended the torture. "Last chance."

Richard fought for breath. "Sub-level C. Three floors down. But it's restricted. You'll never—"

"Not your concern," Thirteen said. "My dear?"

"Gladly." Juniper let go of the man's head. Relief struck Richard, but only for a moment before Juniper swung both fists against his skull. There was no buildup, no torture, just a pure end that silenced the man's wheezing with one fatal blow. Richard crumpled to the ground.

Satisfied, Juniper stepped over him for the back door to the car. Thirteen straightened his collar, then pushed the button for the restricted sub-level. Prompted for keycard access, Juniper returned to the body. She found the card in the dead man's pocket and passed it along.

"Thank you, my sweet," Thirteen said.

The elevator pinged the second the card passed through the scanner. Shifting abruptly, the car began to descend. The journey was quick. At their arrival, Juniper stepped forward—a shield to his person, and for good reason.

When the doors opened, Thirteen found himself face-to-face with a dozen heavily armed guard. They wore full flak jackets and body armor. Shields protected their faces, and all held tight to automatic weapons which came to bear upon the newcomers to the floor.

"Oh, dear," Thirteen said. "Quite the welcoming."

"This is a restricted level," one of the men stated. "There are no authorized visits today. The second you hit that button, you made a world of trouble for yourself."

"Trouble? You must be mistaken. I came for fun." Thirteen's hand patted Juniper's shoulder. He bent close and whispered in her ear. "Show them a good time, Juniper."

"With pleasure."

Screams filled the air. Bodies flew in all directions. Blood spattered the walls and covered the floor. Thirteen remained in the doorway to the elevator. He watched with glee at the carnage unleashed before him, yet saw through it to the wonder that was hidden behind the piling bodies.

Thirteen took a deep breath and prepared for what came next.

# CHAPTER SIXTEEN

Luck had been with the team. In the aftermath of losing June at the airport, the DSA had been struggling to find a lead on their destination. Air traffic control had been given a falsified flight plan. There had been no sign of any unauthorized landings at any national airport during the time of the field team's brief incarceration by local authorities.

It hadn't been until after Morgan had finished her briefing on her experience with Thirteen that the call had come in. The guard at Signet had reached out to the Witness, of all people, with more information about the ID tags procured during the robbery. Each had been location specific and had related to one place in particular: Fort Collins.

No other words between them had been necessary. They had quickly booked a flight to the area, while Adler had started work on a rental van so they could stay mobile once they'd arrived. The silence, however, had remained throughout the flight.

Everyone knew the score: if anything was said, if anyone found the right way into the conversation, it would have steered directly back to the anger and betrayal that ate away at their center.

That was what Metcalf's secrets cost them. Her inability to come forward had broken them as a unit. It was in the disgusted looks, and the morose posture, that carried them to the sleepy Colorado town of Fort Collins.

Every second of silence, Ben wanted to scream for it to change. He needed the DSA back; he needed them whole again. Pure selfishness motivated him: he needed them to find Emily. More than that, however, Ben needed to believe in the work they had been doing. Every thought spoke to their failures, at the lives lost in their wake, and the secrets kept at each turn for some greater good.

Ben swore to be a light to those lost in the dark, but was that even possible anymore? Had they done anything of value with their second chances? The mistakes of the past haunted each of them and tore them apart.

Morgan squeezed the wheel of the rental van. Ben remained ever at her side, not that she noticed. Her focus was on the path ahead.

In the back, Kanigher unveiled the supplies he had gathered shortly after landing. Armaments littered the floor of the cabin, all eyes on him as he pawed through the weaponry.

"Okay," he said. "I know it's not much to look at, but it's all we've got."

Six large weapons made up the bulk of the supplies. Smaller arms were tucked in a bag, along with explosive charges. Night-vision goggles, Kevlar vests, and knives sat in a pile behind Kanigher.

Morgan peered up at the rearview mirror. "Looks like enough."

Ben smirked at the sound of her voice. He hated her silence more than anyone else's. "Did Metcalf give you the company credit card again?"

Kanigher rolled his eyes. "I still have some contacts from my military days." He cringed a bit. "Probably one less after this last-minute request, but if we're really dealing with tree people, we'll need all the help we can get."

"Sticking with tree people?" Ben asked.

Morgan sighed. "I'm not calling them Ents, Riley."

Ben laughed. She always knew the right thing to say. "That hurts, Morgan."

"No Ent would ever do what these monsters are doing," Adler commented. Blank stares showered over her. The mousy analyst rarely piped into the discussion with the field team present. "What? I just read the trilogy again."

"It's true, people," Ben said. "She's an uber-nerd. Except when it comes to the First Family of the Marvel Age of Comics."

Metcalf pinched the bridge of her nose. "Folks? Please?"

The Witness sat back against the seat, his arms across his

chest. "No, really. This is fun to watch."

Ben groaned. "And the joy gets sucked out in an instant. Thanks, Glasses."

Kanigher waited for everyone to settle down once again. Then he lifted one of the weapons from the floor. It was a shotgun, not the typical fare used by the team. "This is —"

"Kanigher," Ben interrupted. "Are we going hunting in the woods or something?"

"Dammit, Riley," Metcalf snapped. "Let the man brief us."

"It's a legitimate question," Ben replied.

Adler shook her head. "It isn't." She reached down to pick up one of the loose shells. "Dragon's Breath, right?"

"With a little more kick to it," Kanigher said with a nod. He stared at Ben. "Incendiary rounds, Riley."

Adler passed the shell over, then took hold of a weapon. Her hands ran across it like an expert. "I haven't seen one of these before. Winchester Super X Pump?"

Kanigher blinked hard, surprised at her knowledge. "That's right. You know your weapons, Adler."

"I'm a multi-purpose geek." She cracked open the shotgun and loaded the chamber. Once in place, Adler snapped the chamber closed. "Single shot, but it should do the job."

"Against tree people?" Ben asked.

"They have superior strength and speed," Kanigher said. He lifted a weapon of his own and loaded it. "We need an edge."

"Doesn't get us in the building," Metcalf said.

Nixon shot up from behind his laptop. "I have some thoughts on that."

They waited for him to start. Instead, there was nothing but the dulcet tones of typing.

Metcalf cleared her throat. "We're all ears, Nixon."

"Right," he said. "If I can set off a containment breach in an isolated portion of the building, I think we can pass you off as Hazmat. There is a storage facility three blocks from the building with the necessary equipment. I can bypass their security, but you'll need to take out the physical guards on site. Probably without the incendiary rounds."

"Nixon," Morgan called from the front seat.

The newcomer to the team continued, his words more and more frantic. "Now, once I tap into their feeds, I can see what

kind of manpower they have for sure. We'll also need a second-
ary team in place for a distraction. I can work up a localized
alarm to draw their attention, and you can pick off any trouble
as they come."

"Nixon!" Morgan yelled.

His focus remained on the screen. "Then there are the locks
on the storage units. It will take some time, but—"

"Will someone shut him up?" Morgan bellowed.

Everyone turned for the front of the van. Metcalf leaned over
the seat. "What is it?"

Adler's eyes grew wide with surprise. "We're here already?"

Nixon shook his head. "But how will we get in?"

"How about the front door?"

Fires burned inside the building. Multiple floors contained
shattered windows. The dead dotted the grounds outside the
entrance in a failed attempt to escape.

Alarms blared within the facility. Sirens rang out in the distance, but at the moment no one guarded the open gate to the
complex.

Nixon stared at the elaborate plan on his screen, then closed
the laptop with a heavy sigh. "Yeah. That works as well, I
guess."

# CHAPTER SEVENTEEN

The team hurried into action the second the van parked. Between Kanigher and Adler, everyone received their care package for entry into the facility. On top of the protective vest and shotgun, all members of the field team were also given a breathing unit.

Metcalf tried to hold back her pride. There was a threat inside the CDC office and the team prepared to handle it. No questions asked.

She rounded up the crew at the back of the van. "I want two teams," she announced. "We might have the blueprints Nixon was able to get for us, but we don't know where our targets will be stationed. We'll need to sweep floor by floor to find these guys. I'll take Kanigher to the lower levels, while Morgan and Ben—"

"No," Morgan interrupted.

Metcalf fell back a step. "No?"

"I'll call the play," Morgan said.

"That's not necessary," Metcalf replied. "I can—"

"Take a seat," Morgan shot at her. "This is fieldwork, and we are the field team. You're welcome to come along, but you play by our rules."

All pride in her team vanished. Metcalf wanted the fight. There wasn't time for the debate, though. Metcalf threw her hands up in surrender and made her way to the open back doors of the van. She plopped down on the edge, a nod thrown back to the waiting team.

"Okay," Morgan said. "She's right about needing two teams. Ben and Kanigher can take the upper floors, while we—"

"Morgan." Ben cut her off. "Let me."

"Ben?"

His eyes met hers, then both turned to meet their irritated superior, who waited to see which team would pick her. "I'll take Metcalf to the lower levels."

Morgan bit her lower lip. Slowly, she nodded. "Fine. You've got Ben."

"Wonderful," Metcalf said, pushing off the back of the van. "Any other suggestions?"

"Quite a few, actually," Morgan snapped. "But we're pressed for time."

"I'd be happy to help," the Witness said with a hand raised.

Eyes shot his way, and all uttered the same stern response. "No."

Metcalf strapped on her vest. She primed her shotgun and locked a few shells beneath the barrel for easy access. Then she grabbed a handful and jammed them into the pockets on the front of her vest.

The sirens closed in on them. They needed to breach the building before they arrived, or a whole new dilemma would take over. Metcalf had already been through enough in Millington. The time for delays was over.

She turned to the analysts on the team. "Adler's in charge out here. Take the van and find a quiet corner. I don't want you engaging with anyone, and I mean anyone." Metcalf caught Morgan's glare from the corner of her eye. "That is, if everyone else is okay with that decision?"

Morgan's fist clenched tight by her side. "You are such a piece of —"

"We're good with it!" Nixon put a hand to his chest, his smile completely out of place. "I mean, I am. Good with it, that is." He turned to Adler. "You're good with it too, right?"

Adler gave an awkward look and nodded.

Nixon breathed a sigh of relief. He shifted in front of the Witness. "And you?" Silence was his only response. Nixon shook his head in understanding. "Yeah, that doesn't really matter, does it?"

Nixon climbed into the back of the van. He pumped his fist into the air. "Go team."

Adler quickly slammed the doors shut in his face. Morgan

tossed her the keys to the van. The Witness offered them nothing, not a sign of what was ahead, not a damn clue what Thirteen wanted within the building.

His silence was damning, not only to himself but to Metcalf, who had backed his intentions for so long only to be burned by them time and time again. Instead of ably assisting their efforts, he stonewalled them at every turn.

The Witness fixed his glasses to his face. He rounded the van for the passenger side.

"I feel good about this," Ben chuckled. "Everyone else?"

Morgan slapped him on the arm. Kanigher barely gave Metcalf a second glance; he focused on the burning building before them.

Metcalf lifted her weapon. "Grab your gear. We breach in two minutes."

# CHAPTER EIGHTEEN

Metcalf's two-minute warning left her waiting. The unknown stood before her, threatening to upend any control left to her. There was no pattern to Thirteen, and according to Morgan's briefing, there wouldn't be, not with a man who only cared to leave chaos in his wake. That made things even tenser for her.

While the others gathered up their equipment, Metcalf rounded the van. The Witness remained along the side. He leaned comfortably against the door, his hands tucked behind his head.

"I should come with you," he said at her approach.

"Not going to happen," Metcalf snapped.

"You don't understand—"

She grabbed him by the collar. Twisting about, Metcalf pushed the enigmatic man away from the van and into the nearby fence. The chain rattled behind him, yet the Witness made no move to escape her grasp. He didn't blink in terror at her assault, merely stared at her like a damn automaton rather than a human being.

It sent her reeling. A scream unleashed, Metcalf slammed him against the chain, then threw him to the side. The Witness staggered slightly but maintained his feet. Metcalf, however, wanted to crumble to the ground.

Her frustration nearly did her in. She had trusted the man. She had put her faith in what he'd shared over the years—the secrets the two of them had kept from the world. Then Bellbrook happened. With it came betrayal and a new secret to hold. Now, that lie of omission threatened her mission… and her team.

"Metcalf?" Ben called from the van. "It's time."

"I need a minute."

"But—"

Metcalf spun to face her worried agent. "One minute."

Kanigher caught her anger and nodded. He pulled Riley ahead. "We'll secure the lobby. See you inside."

Morgan said nothing, yet her silence spoke volumes. It always had between them. Morgan had become their moral compass over the years, and Metcalf had come to trust her judgment more than most. She had led Metcalf to help save Ben's life at the risk of their mission. Morgan's influence had convinced Metcalf to open the doors to the Bunker to more personnel, for a better shot at success in the future. The agent's judgment had also come at a cost, though. It had opened the door to this: to the Witness' secrets coming to light.

Metcalf needed something in return. "What is it?"

"Susan, while I understand your anger, there is no need—"

Metcalf brought her hands up. She moved to throttle the man, then paused. "Dammit!" Her fist slammed into the mesh at his back. The metal chain snapped back and forth from the blow. The Witness didn't bother to flinch. He held no fear of her. "I need to know."

"What?"

She pointed at the building. "What is he doing in there?"

"Again, Susan, I'm afraid I have no idea."

She couldn't read him. His hidden eyes helped conceal any deception. His voice did the rest, never wavering and never giving anything away.

"Cut the crap," she spat. Her backup sidearm slipped from the holster into her palm, and she turned it on him. "Tell me now."

"Susan, there is no reason for this."

The gun inched toward his temple. "I know who you are. I know what you are, what you've always been. Whether you've seen it that way doesn't matter, but to me, you've been a source of seemingly limitless information: a witness to everything somehow. So I'll ask again. What is this Clevinger doing here?"

The Witness secured his glasses to his face. Light beamed from beneath the lenses, but faded just as quickly. "I do not know."

Metcalf's finger tightened on the trigger. "We are putting our lives on the line. We deserve the truth."

"And I am giving it to you." Jaw clenched, the Witness spun toward her. He snatched the gun before him. Holding tight to the barrel, he lowered it from his face. "It's all changed. What we've done over the years with the building of the DSA? The Trust stepping out of the shadows years ahead of schedule and with David Hollis at its head?" He shook his head, dropping the gun. A soft huff of breath left him, his stoic voice no longer quite as assured as it once had been. "Those were seismic shifts, but even the smaller ones have mattered in the grand scheme of things. Like Benjamin's recruitment. And yes, even Bellbrook. Everything we have done, what I have done, was to change the future... and it has. I don't hold all the answers anymore, Susan."

The gun fell away. It was why he had brought them to Millington in the first place, to show them what his time in Bellbrook had wrought. None of it had been planned, none of it seen ahead of time, despite the knowledge he maintained. The future was cut off from him — his future.

It scared the living hell out of her.

"I no longer know for certain what comes next, Susan."

They were on their own. For the first time in their dubious relationship, they stood on equal footing when it came to the unknown. However, he continued to hold something back.

"Tell me the rest of it," she said matter-of-factly.

"I don't—"

She raised the pistol once more. "I have listened to you for far too long. Long enough to know when you're holding back on me. What is Thirteen after in there?"

"How would I know, Susan?" the Witness said. He leaned forward, letting the gun settle along his forehead. "I just told you—"

"The virus he's after," she interjected. "When the guard at Signet mentioned a virus, you immediately stepped in and sidetracked him. What do they have that is so dangerous?"

"Something I had hoped was lost in a deep, dark pit or burned from existence," the Witness answered. He settled against the fencing. "While I may not be able to see everything to come, I do recall one thing. This facility is where they kept Oliver Blake's nanovirus."

"Blake... You mean..."

"The virus that killed Agent Grissom—the first time, at any rate—is inside that building," the Witness said. "I believe that to be Thirteen's true target."

# CHAPTER NINETEEN

The lobby was a tomb. Ben led the way through, his breather tight over his mouth and nose. A tube connected to a small tank at his side that reminded him of a respirator in a hospital.

At least in a hospital, there was a chance for survival. Here, only the dead remained. They lay where they fell, at their stations or in the middle of the floor. The scanning belt that led the way deeper into the lobby continued to run, though it was obstructed by two guards — one at each end.

Boils and pustules covered their exposed skin. Blood ran from tear ducts. Whatever viral agent took their lives was fierce and efficient. None went quietly, their screams permanently on display in death.

Morgan and Kanigher stuck close. Without verbal communication, they relied on visual cues and scanned to cover the enormity of the open space at the front of the building.

The lobby was two-stories tall and fed into an elevator bank near the rear. Security offices dominated most of the space. The monitors were seen through small rectangular windows along the upper half of the doors.

At Morgan's motioning, Ben moved for the closed doors. He tried each in turn. The majority were regular offices, the frame of the door never quite connecting with the thin carpeting. The toxin loosed by Thirteen had no trouble finding its way into each room and killing the occupants.

However, at the far end of the row stood a thicker door sealed off, with no gap at its base. A rectangular window decorated the door, the same as the rest, and Ben stood on his toes for a better view inside.

A head shot up on the other side of the glass. The shock near-ly caused Ben's breathing unit to slip from his lips. He staggered back and almost tumbled into a concerned Morgan. When they both found their footing, they turned for the window, and the wide eyes washing over them.

"The lever!" the man within shouted. The thick door muted his words, but they made them out with some effort. His finger jabbed at the window. "You have to release the lever to filter out the toxin!"

They found the lever in question along the far wall. Morgan rushed over first. Pushing through the bodies with care, Morgan entered the security suite on the opposite side of the scanning belt. She flipped open a hatch that interlocked the ventilation system with a single computer. The screen flashed red, identify-ing the deadly toxin in the air, unable to compensate without manual assistance.

Lowering down the lever released the hold on the system. Giant fans whirred to life overhead and throughout the floor. They pulled the diseased air out, while a fresh supply was brought into the room. The entire floor was flushed and replen-ished in a matter of sixty seconds.

The man in the window gave them the thumbs up when the task was accomplished. Ben, however, remained cautious and continued to enjoy his breathing unit. It wasn't until the lock on the door gave way and the man stepped into the lobby that relief filled Ben's face.

"Thank you!" the man cheered. "I was doing routine mainte-nance when the toxin registered. I tried…" He glanced around at the dead. They were his colleagues and friends. The weight of his loss caused his knees to buckle, and he fell to the carpet. Tears poured down his cheeks.

Ben removed his breather. His hand settled on the man's shoulder. "There was nothing you could have done."

"I tried…" the man sobbed. "I wanted to… to help, but it was too late."

Ben crouched beside him. "I'm sorry about what happened. Why didn't they activate the flush when the system called for it?"

The man wiped at his running nose. Pushing through the tears, he struggled his way to his feet. "They couldn't." He pointed to the dead closest to the security suite. On top of the violent deaths inflicted upon them by Thirteen's virus, they also bore clear injuries and broken bones. Arms were snapped and hung limply at their sides. Their legs were twisted awkwardly beneath them. "There were these two guys—huge guys—and they blocked security from acting. I don't know why the toxin didn't affect them."

*Because they were from Bellbrook,* Ben thought immediately. Morgan and Kanigher agreed without a word. They had found three trees in Millington. All three subjects were in the building with them.

"Any clue where they are?"

The man nodded, then waved the agents toward the security suite. "Yeah," he replied, using his keycard for access. "Security tracks all badges from this room. Not too many mobile now, but look."

The monitor was clear. Two bodies were moving below, and two above.

"Guess we're still splitting up," Morgan grumbled.

"Where are we heading?" Metcalf asked from the door.

Ben shot a look at the man. "Sir?"

"Michael," the man said. "Michael Nesbitt. There's a bit of interference. The exact position isn't coming through like it should, but I'd say the restricted level below."

"That's us," Metcalf said. Ben nodded, but waited.

"You'll need an ID from security."

Morgan crouched over the closest body on the floor. She pulled the badge from the man's shirt and tossed it to Ben.

"Done and done," he said. "Where are the others?"

"Somewhere on the 18th or 19th floor." Michael slammed his hand against the terminal. The screen flickered. The information failed to change. "They must be messing with one of the server rooms, but I can't tell—"

"It's okay," Morgan said. "We'll take care of it."

"Yeah." Michael rubbed at his neck. "But who the hell are you people?"

"Great question," Ben said. "Morgan?"

"We're here to help," Morgan answered. "I need you to talk to the police approaching and keep the perimeter of this building secured."

"Just the perimeter? But —"

"We don't know what other surprises they have in store," Morgan continued.

"Won't stop them," Michael said in a small voice. "And those aren't police coming — well, most of them won't be at any rate."

"What do you mean?"

"This is the CDC," he replied. "The second the toxin was identified, every federal agency in the city heard about it and headed our way. They have orders to take the building and use whatever force necessary to secure both it and anyone inside."

"Secure?" Ben asked. "Let me guess. Not with a great, big hug?"

"Not so much."

Morgan rolled her eyes. "A time limit. Perfect."

"Do what you can for us, Michael," Ben said. "We're not the bad guys here."

Michael nodded. Morgan helped him toward the exit, then joined them at the stairs.

"No elevator?"

"Too risky," Metcalf replied. "Same for us."

"Not as much of a jaunt," Morgan remarked. Ben's grin told her who she sounded like with the comment. "Never mind."

"Be careful." Kanigher started his way up the steps.

"Morgan," Ben called.

"You too," she said without looking. They rounded the corner, their steps echoing in the distance.

"Ready?" Metcalf said.

Ben gripped his shotgun tight. "Here we go."


They made it down a single level before Ben stopped.

Metcalf tumbled against him. "What is it?"

Her breath ran across his neck, and Ben shuffled down the remaining flight before turning to face her. "We should have stuck together."

Metcalf shook her head. "You heard that man back there. Two threats. Two groups."

"Doesn't matter," Ben replied. "Backup is on the way."

"Not the kind that will help us." Metcalf joined him on the small landing. Her hand reached for his shoulder. "They have no idea what they are getting into by breaching this facility."

"Like we did?" Ben said. "Fine. So, they don't know about what happened in Bellbrook. So they don't understand tree people, or whatever we're calling them. But isn't that the point? They *should* know about them. They should know about all of it!"

For a moment, Metcalf appeared ready to answer his ramblings. They were alone and had been since the DSA's fall. It was an action brought on by her, and she read the thought clearly on his face.

"Say it," she said. Her words carried her down the steps to the restricted level. "Go on, Ben. Get it off your chest. Everyone else has today."

"Can you blame them?" They rounded the final landing, then paused before the door. "I told you this would happen. I gave you a chance to set this right. To show everyone how you've changed, but you haven't, have you? You can't."

"Like you've ever trusted me," she said with a harsh laugh. "Or anyone else, for that matter. Or does Morgan know about the files you have from Wesley Fuller and the photo he gave you of the Witness?"

*How did she know?* He hadn't told anyone. Morgan suspected; she had read his hesitancy back in Millington, but he held the secret from her and the rest. He hadn't been sure how or what to share, and that decision had done little to help in their current situation. Still, Metcalf's knowledge of his personal inquiries staggered him.

"See?" he said. "That's exactly my point."

"You don't even know your point anymore," Metcalf spat back.

"Wrong," Ben said. "It's about trust. It's always about trust with you. You've given me no reason to place mine in you, yet I stayed to try to make this not about you, or us, but about doing some good in the world. Are we though?"

Metcalf ignored him. She moved for the door. Ben wheeled around her and cut her off. "Hey!" She stopped shy of his hand. His eyes pleaded with her. "Are we doing any good at all?"

"How can you—"

"Emily is still out there somewhere," he continued. "The Trust is everywhere, cutting us off from our friends, family, and any kind of potential ally we might find. We're locked in that damn bunker, practically hiding from the world, and you don't have a problem with any of that?"

"We are doing good here, Ben," she said in a calm voice. "You have to see that."

"All I see is you barking orders and making decisions." Ben's gaze fell to the floor. He kicked at the ground between them. "Each one affects us all now, Metcalf. And they won't fall when you do. They'll just leave. Then where will you be?"

Metcalf pushed through him. She held out her hand. Ben sighed and removed the borrowed ID card. She snatched it from him and let the scanner by the door read the barcode. The lock clicked, and the door released from the frame.

Before opening it, Metcalf turned back to him. "I'll deal with them, Ben. Now come on. We have to stop Thirteen before it's too late."

Another order. Ben shook his head, curious if Metcalf had heard a damn word he'd said to her. He wondered if it would even matter in the end.

"Yes, ma'am."

# CHAPTER TWENTY

The climb went quickly. Morgan and Kanigher worked in silence, the sound of their breath the only accompaniment to their stomping feet up the steps. Eighteen flights went by in a blink due to their focus.

For Morgan, it was a pleasant change of pace from the usual banter shared with Ben. She appreciated the camaraderie, but after everything that had happened over the last two days, she was grateful for the reprieve from more lies and secrets.

She rushed through the door, skirting right while Kanigher took the left. Back to back, the pair moved along the winding hall of the building. Bodies lay scattered around them. The air had been cleansed, but the damage done by the virus remained self-evident. The place was a massive grave, a tragedy no one would ever truly understand in the end.

Outside, the sun waned in the distance. Morgan couldn't believe another day had passed by. The case had consumed them from the start. More than that, the drama underneath the situation—the piece that threatened to pull them all down the rabbit hole—continued to loom whenever she stopped to think for too long.

Instead, she kept her mind on the task at hand. Michael had pointed to the server room on two different floors. The one on the 18th was clearly labeled. Morgan used a stolen badge to gain access—there were plenty to choose from during their travels. She found emptiness inside.

"Dammit," she cursed. Pushing through Kanigher, she started back for the stairs and another climb.

Kanigher's footfalls followed quickly. At the base of the

stairs, he called after her. "Want to talk about it?"

Morgan paused at the landing between floors. The shotgun in her grip fell to her side, and her shoulders slumped slightly. "It should have been me. Not Riley."

Kanigher joined her on the landing. An eyebrow cocked at her remark.

"I have quite a few things to say to Metcalf," Morgan clarified.

Kanigher nodded. "Yeah. I think we all do. Probably why Riley made the call. Safer for all involved."

Morgan knew it to be true. She had been with Metcalf too long not to have bumped heads, but this felt different. This wasn't a superior compartmentalizing information for the good of the mission. This was more personal and had been ever since they struck out on their own. The weight of their task was too great to falter now.

"She's damaging the mission, Kanigher," Morgan said. She climbed up the remaining steps. "Splitting the team when we need to stand together."

"I agree," Kanigher said at her side. "Doesn't mean she'll listen to me any more than the rest of you."

"This doesn't work apart. We break, and the Trust wins." Morgan let out a long breath, her hand tight to the railing. Her gaze fell to the floor. "They win, and none of us gets to go home. To live our lives again. To see our families again."

She hadn't realized how much that fact bothered her until she said it out loud. She hadn't spoken to her sister-in-law in weeks. Charlotte had been her lifeline back into her brother's life, yet since their retreat into the Bunker, Morgan had not received a single update about her brother's mental health. His last bout of depression had resulted in a suicide attempt during the holidays. She had been lucky enough to be there, to help in some small way to comfort her family in their time of need. But now?

Morgan missed them. She worried about their well-being over her own.

"Kid?" Kanigher asked, clearly reading her thoughts.

"Nephew," Morgan answered.

Kanigher nodded. He finished the climb, then stopped at the door. "Three nieces."

"You?"

"Surprising, I know," he said with a laugh. "They are my three angels in a world of devils. I do this for them. Makes the fight mean more that way."

It certainly did. Somehow, just picturing her nephew's face gave Morgan the strength to finish her climb.

She gripped tight to the shotgun, then turned to Kanigher. "This isn't going to end well, is it?"

"Probably not." Kanigher opened the door, his weapon in front of him. "Ready?"

Morgan took the lead once more. She cleared the first corridor. More bodies surrounded them, but didn't carry the silence that had trailed their movements throughout the rest of the building. Shuffling feet caused the agents to slow their approach. Morgan took to the corner and shimmied low. Slipping a mirror from her vest, she placed it out in the open for a glimpse of what was waiting for them around the bend.

Two men exited the server room. They carried no weapons, nor did they need to. Their bodies were built like trucks, the suits ill-fitted against their massive frames. They appeared to be heading in the other direction when a stray beam of sunlight caught the mirror. It reflected toward the pair, who caught sight of the random light from the corner of their eyes.

They turned to greet Morgan. Bloodlust sat in their black, beady eyes.

Morgan dropped the mirror and raised her weapon. "Dammit. I knew I should have gone with Metcalf."

# CHAPTER TWENTY-ONE

The restricted level opened up into a massive laboratory. Security lay in pieces near the doorway. Blood stained the floor. The soldiers, heavily armed and in full riot gear, had been torn through viscerally. Limbs lay detached among the dead. Terror marked their wide stares. They hadn't fallen from some viral agent: they had been slaughtered.

Metcalf stepped over one, a nod to Ben to watch his step as they moved deeper into the lab. Testing stations were positioned throughout. Large tables contained advanced chemistry sets, mixtures of chemicals bubbling like some apothecary's hut instead of a high-tech agency like the CDC. Computers ran diagnostics, and machines clicked and whirred with each analysis.

Vials sat in refrigeration units along the left-hand side. Hundreds of specimens, all labeled in bold print, lay in full view from the main floor. If just one made its way out, there would be untold devastation.

Metcalf's steps quickened with the thought. A lone figure stood at the end of the units. He carried an opaque vial, the name BLAKE in bold letters along the side.

The Witness had been right, as always. Metcalf raised her weapon. "Drop it!"

The figure was slow to turn. Tall and thin, with sunken cheeks, the man wore a light jacket over a shirt and tie. Mania filled his eyes, aglow with the potential found in the room. He kept a death grip on the vial.

"I would rather not," Thirteen said with a sinister sneer.

Ben shifted closer, weapon at the ready. Sweat dotted his brow. His concern over Thirteen was clear. "Do it, or so help me…"

Thirteen tossed the vial between his hands. With each toss, the agents dropped back a step. Their fear gave him more room to maneuver through the restricted level. "Do you havez any idea the potential I hold here? The virus within this tube could annihilate ten city blocks in a day. The state would fall in a week. Such chaos. It's enough to give me chills."

"Why, Clevinger?" Metcalf asked through gritted teeth.

Thirteen caught the vial. His fingers squeezed against the tubing. "How I hate that name."

Ben shot her a look. He didn't have to. She knew the moment she said the name, she had made a tactical error. However, Ben asked for more with his sharp glare—an ounce of trust to handle the situation. She nodded his way.

Thirteen read their trepidation. His anger melted with a long breath, and the smirk returned. "Apologies. I have some issues with my so-called father. We all have our burdens to bear, I imagine. Like yours, for instance."

"What?"

Ben's eyes widened. He spun toward her. "Metcalf, look out!"

June leaped from the shadows. She crashed to the floor from above, her hands extended like claws. Metcalf jumped back and collided with a lab terminal. Beakers smashed. Liquid contents seeped along the ground, causing steam to rise and an acrid smell to permeate the level.

Even with the dead surrounding them, nothing came close to preparing Metcalf for June's attack. The Bellbrook survivor's body was immense, her skin hardened and bumpy like chainmail more than human flesh.

Raising her shotgun to confront June, Metcalf prepared to fire. "This doesn't have to go this way. Don't make me—"

June's arm shot out. Fingers extended like growing branches of a tree. They snarled around Metcalf's wrist and pulled Metcalf forward. The shotgun fell low. Metcalf struggled to correct her aim, but lost her footing in the melee. June swung out. The back of her arm connected with Metcalf's side and sent her careening over a lab station and to the floor.

"No!" Ben cried. He tucked his head down and charged at the woman. He wrapped his arms around her, squeezed tight around her midsection, then drove her toward the wall. "This isn't you, June. He's controlling you. He's—"

Hands fell on Ben's shoulders. She ripped him loose from her body. With ease, she lifted him to meet his frightened eyes. A wicked smile grew on her face. "He's letting me have fun."

"Crap."

Tendrils wrapped around his neck and squeezed. With her other hand, June slapped Ben across the cheek. Blood squirted between his lips. Another slap caused his cheek to swell; his vision on the right side went dark.

"Ben!" Metcalf scrambled to her feet. Shells from the shotgun scattered around her. Frantically grabbing a handful, she tucked them away and leveled her weapon. "Put him down!"

"Not yet." June was enthralled with the man in her grip. Her fingers lengthened along his neck, wrapping over and over again in an ever-growing noose. Death was the only thing that could appease her.

"Shoot... her," Ben muttered. The strain caused his face to redden. He kicked out at June, to no avail. His fingers failed to pry the tendrils from his throat.

"I can't," Metcalf said with a shake of her head. "You're too close."

Ben's eyes pleaded.

"You'll burn," Metcalf said.

"Metcalf!" Ben roared, fighting for breath. "Trust... me. Trust... someone!"

She didn't need any further prompting. Metcalf slammed down on the trigger. Braced against her shoulder, the recoil still nearly toppled her. The shell slammed into the side of June and exploded in a blaze. June's entire side lit up; her body burned from head to toe.

A repugnant scream erupted from the Bellbrook survivor. Pain and anguish mixed with fury. The branches tight to Ben's neck finally gave way thanks to the rising flames. The fire singed his arms and legs as Ben struggled for freedom. He fell to the ground with a thud, but the menace of June continued to loom over him.

"No," the changed woman said. Ashes rose from her burning figure, her face charred from the blast. She grabbed for Ben, murderous intent in her eyes. "I'm not finished with you yet."

"Yes, you are." Metcalf jammed another shell into place. She took aim and fired. The Dragon's Breath connected with the Bellbrook survivor's back. Flames spread from the impact site. June screamed, consumed by the raging fire.

Metcalf stood in wait. She cracked open the barrel of the shotgun and slipped in another shell. The gun was ready; her focus never wavered from the smoldering ashes spread along the floor.

Satisfied the threat was over, Metcalf moved for Ben. "Are you all right?"

He took her extended hand. "Yeah, I'm…" Shuffling to his feet, Ben almost fell back to the floor. She pulled him closer to support his weight. "Oh, boy. I'm okay. I am."

She looked him over. Scrapes covered his arms, along with several minor burns. The right side of his face was dismal, but when she shifted to the left, she noticed the fear in his eye.

"What is it?"

"Thirteen!"

The maniac slammed into Metcalf. The shotgun fell from her grip. Ben tried to bolster her, but his strength was not up to the challenge. He tumbled to the ground. His head slammed hard against the tile and he stopped moving. Metcalf caught herself on the side of a nearby table. She spun to greet her attacker.

Thirteen loomed over June's ashes. The virus was still in his hands. "My poor Juniper. You took her from me."

"Don't pretend you cared," Metcalf said. "She was a puppet for you to manipulate."

A nod of acceptance passed from him. He wiped at false tears. "She still deserved better," he said with a sigh. "Oh well. Perhaps I'll dedicate a mass slaughter to her or something."

Thirteen started for the elevator. He continued to toss the virus between his hands, but Metcalf no longer cared about the threat within the vial. Blake's name on the label meant nothing to her. All that mattered was stopping Thirteen.

"Don't even think about it." Metcalf dove at him, hands outstretched. Thirteen's steps quickened, but he failed to clear her reach as she grabbed hold of his legs.

Thirteen lost his footing. The vial flew into the air. "You fool! The virus!"

Metcalf watched it fall. She knocked Thirteen aside, then

kicked up from the floor after the viral agent. The vial hit her hand and bounded back into the air for a brief second before she snatched it. She cradled the deadly agent against her like a newborn as she crashed to the floor.

For a brief second, Metcalf thought it was all over—that the virus had infected her just as it had Grissom so many months earlier. Everything she'd fought for evaporated in one act, and the mission ended the only way she knew it would: with her death.

Slowly, Metcalf opened her eyes. The vial was intact, the contents within still locked away. A sigh of relief escaped her.

Thirteen was already on his feet again. Instead of moving for the elevator or the stairs, he stood at the computers.

"My hero," he said. His fingers continued to work, his vengeful gaze locked on the screen.

"You monster." Metcalf struggled to find her feet, the vial slowing her every move. "You would have murdered thousands, all to get back at your deranged daddy?"

His hands slammed on the keyboard. "Yes!" he shouted. "Thousands upon thousands. The number is meaningless. He set me on this path, then condemned me for it. He made me, shaped me, molded me, and then rejected me. I would see the whole world burn to show him the truth!"

"The truth?"

"That I was right!" Thirteen bellowed. He sounded like a petulant child throwing a tantrum. "My work, my vision for humanity, is the only way forward."

"You're insane."

"Insane thoughts forged the world," he replied. "Creation is taking the unbelievable and forcing it upon dullards and ingrates. Then it becomes a notion of pure brilliance. You'll see. Just like him. Just like Howard… When I am finished, this entire world will see."

Metcalf clutched tight to the virus. "Never going to happen. Not with this."

"That?" Thirteen said with a laugh. "Oliver Blake might have been considered a genius, but he was nothing compared to what I have planned."

"What?" Metcalf asked. That was the goal, wasn't it? To steal Blake's work, a nanovirus capable of killing the population of an entire restaurant in a manner of seconds? Wasn't that why Thirteen was here in the first place? "Then why—"

"Consider him a good starting point. I'll find another." He left the computer, twisting dials on components throughout the lab. "Truly, my dear, there are so many more vile ways to go. I know them all. Like say, asphyxiation?"

His fist slammed down on a red control along the wall. Alarms buzzed in every corner. Emergency lighting showered the room in crimson as glass barriers dropped on all sides of the lab.

"Ben!" Metcalf called as the walls fell into place. He still lay on the floor, cut off by the barrier. Metcalf beat her open hand against the glass separating them.

"He can't hear you," Thirteen said. "Not with the fan running."

"Fan?"

Giant blades whirred to life overhead. Ben woke at the sound, clearly confused by his predicament. He tried to speak, but her name caught on his lips. Fear kicked in as recognition took hold. His hands shot to his throat. He couldn't breathe.

"I give him a minute before the fan sucks all the air from the room," Thirteen said. He moved for the exit, his steps casual and unafraid. "He'll die gasping, begging to be saved."

"Open it," Metcalf demanded. She reached for her sidearm, only to find an empty holster waiting for her.

"Looking for this?" Thirteen held out her pistol. He must have grabbed it during their struggle. Dropping it to the ground, he kicked it away from her and out of sight. Thirteen wagged his finger at her, in full control of the situation. "Save him or stop me. There isn't time for both."

# CHAPTER TWENTY-TWO

Adler parked on the far side of the lot, away from the building between several other cars to throw off any suspicion. As she completed the task, flashing lights beamed throughout the area. Black SUVs accompanied local law enforcement as they took over the entire entryway like a massive cordon.

Adler watched a man flee from the building. Hands flailing in the air, the man rushed to the leader of the operation. Explanations passed between them as the frantic figure pointed repeatedly toward the building.

Adler understood the warning immediately. He had clearly been in contact with Metcalf and the others and had been passing along a message from them. It meant little in the end. The leader waved the man down while ordering his team into position. All wore flak jackets and carried semi-automatics. They breached moments later, unafraid for their lives. Their only concern was for the contents locked within the complex.

The waiting game took over after that. It wasn't Adler's favorite, and she found it difficult to monitor local chatter with the blank stare of the Witness at her back. Eventually, she closed her laptop and shuffled out of her seat. The Witness remained locked on her, even as she checked on Nixon. Her companion continued to work. Nixon somehow always kept working.

"Someone just exited the back of the building," he commented under his breath.

No eyes monitored that side of the property. The agents had yet to secure that exit, their focus on the front. Adler shifted closer to Nixon. "Any idea who they might be?"

"I don't have a visual," Nixon said. "Cameras are down, but

the door sensor was triggered. Someone definitely made it out of there."

"We should investigate." The Witness' voice boomed within the cabin of the van. All other noise faded in an instant, as if his very presence demanded their full attention.

Adler hesitated, then shook her head. "We stay here. I don't want to take us out of position in case we're needed for a quick evac."

The Witness did not comment. He merely folded his hands in his lap. The opaque lenses continued to stare through her. From behind them, reflecting off the windows of the van, Adler noticed a light emanating. It was dim, but clear, thanks to the fading sun.

Nixon nodded at her decision. Placing the laptop down for a moment, he reached for a fresh bottle of Pepsi. He offered some to Adler, who lifted the water bottle at her side for a long swig. Satisfaction achieved, Adler set down the bottle. The Witness' blank eyes took in her every move.

"What are they exactly?" she asked, unable to ignore the Witness any longer. "Your glasses?"

"What do you mean?" he replied in an intrigued tone.

"They aren't corrective." Adler leaned close to study the glasses. "I've seen screens like those before. Are they information receptacles? Some form of digital interface, maybe? How are they powered? How do they operate?"

The Witness settled against his seat. Slowly, he lifted his hand to the arm of his glasses. The light grew the moment he slipped them from his face. They were screens. Telemetry and data scrolled in thin lines on each side—almost like a heads-up display. But that wasn't the fascinating part of the revelation. It was the Witness' eyes that drew their full attention the moment they were visible. Both had been scarred over, the sockets visibly destroyed by some kind of trauma.

Nixon yelped at the sight of the man's lack of eyes. "Holy!"

Adler winced at his reaction, silencing him without a word. She shifted her chair closer to the man, fascinated. "The glasses are your eyes, aren't they? Incredible."

Somehow, their presence gave the man his sight back. There didn't appear to be any input into the man's visual cortex, yet the glasses provided the Witness with everything he needed to get around in the world… and more.

The data fed through the lenses was extensive. Adler tried to keep up, to note the patterns, but they weren't straightforward. Most were cryptic symbols, but to the Witness, their meaning was clear.

He put the glasses back in place. His lips curled. "I'm impressed. What was your name again?"

The question stunned Adler. "You seem to know quite a bit about us, but you don't know my name?"

"Remind an old man."

She found the comment funny, and they shared a soft chuckle. The Witness didn't appear to be much older than Ben, more than likely a contemporary of Metcalf. There was nothing old about him.

"It's Adler," she said. "Alison Adler."

"Really?" The light behind the lenses flared for an instant, then faded. "How strange."

"Strange?" It was not the word she would have used to describe the exchange. The man appeared to know everything about everyone. His inability to identify her caused a wave of concern to wash over her. "You really don't know me, do you?"

"Not in the least," the Witness said with a sharp voice. He shifted quickly in his seat toward their companion in the van. "Now him? I know Nixon Jessup very well."

Nixon stopped working at the mention of his name. "Me?"

"The smartest man in the room," the Witness continued. "Or at least what he professes to be."

"Because it tends to be true," Nixon retorted. He glanced at Adler and offered a sympathetic shrug. "No offense."

"None taken."

The Witness cleared his throat and leaned closer. "You find angles through systems and people in the same manner. You treat them alike, detached."

"Now that's not—"

"I'm not faulting your intelligence," the Witness said, a dismissive wave at the need for any response. "Only that it will fail you in the end. For the man who sees all the angles, you won't see the betrayal coming until it is far too late."

"Betrayal?" Adler asked. "What betrayal?"

The Witness ignored her words and her presence, locked on

Nixon. "You need to stay detached. You need to trust in your first instinct or you won't see the end of this journey."

"What do you —"

"Hold it," Nixon said. "Are you talking about my death?"

Adler shook her head. "No one's dying."

"Are you sure about that?"

"Am I dying?" Nixon chimed in, a hand to his forehead. "I do feel a little flush, but I assumed it was being in this van."

"Nixon." Adler caught his worried gaze and smiled. "He's messing with you. That's what he does. Agent Riley said the same thing about their first meeting."

"Yeah?" Nixon relaxed at her nod. Anger filled his face, and he pointed to the Witness. "Don't do that to people."

"Instead of needling my colleague, how about providing some actual support for this mission?" Adler said. "Show us your stuff. Save the day."

"That's why we're here."

"Then how do we stop Thirteen?"

The Witness turned toward the building. "We don't."

She wanted to press him for something they could use, but fell silent for the moment. A quick look to Nixon put them back on their respective tasks. There was chatter to monitor and intel to feed the team as it came through. No word came from within, and no clue how this would end. The Witness refused to give them a clear sign, leaving Adler with the only thing left to her: her innate ability to hope for the best.

# CHAPTER TWENTY-THREE

They were overwhelmed immediately. Morgan and Kanigher tried to withdraw, to find some cover from the charging pair of Bellbrook survivors, but found themselves overtaken right out of the gate.

"Kanigher, look—"

A hand belted him across the face. The stalwart agent left the ground for an instant and crashed against the inner wall. All his focus remained on holding tight to his shotgun.

Morgan lifted her own in defense. Every movement felt sluggish compared to their attackers. The Bellbrook Batch batted at her. With each swipe of their claw-like fingers, Morgan reeled away from them. She staggered toward the stairwell, looking for an opening to take her shot.

"Come on," she muttered. "Come on!"

The bang of the weapon boomed in her ears. She fell hard to the ground from the recoil. The shot, however, missed its target. Soaring between the pair, the shell collided with the window opposite Kanigher and exploded in a ball of fire. Shards of glass sprayed the outside wall, and small pieces scattered along the floor.

She pumped the shotgun to eject the spent round. Before she could reload, the man on her right grabbed hold of her weapon. Fingers spread like branches. They wrapped up the shotgun and squeezed. The weapon cracked into pieces and crumbled before her like a tinker-toy.

"Shit."

Her attacker launched at her, fury in his eyes. Morgan rolled out of range of the assault, then pushed up to her feet in a hurry.

She braced for impact as she saw the man rush toward her shoulder first. He collided with her, putting all his weight into the blow — a significant amount considering the bulk he carried because of his transformation. Air slipped from her lungs, and the force of the strike made it impossible to replenish. The wrapped bandage around her midsection gave way, and her injuries screamed for attention.

The Bellbrook man carried her down the corridor. When her assailant skidded to a halt, Morgan continued and slammed her back into the wall with a thud. She fell to her knees, hoping to catch her breath. Tendrils snaked around her neck. They lifted her into the air. The man's eyes washed over her with pure ecstasy. He wanted the kill.

"Kanigher..." she gasped.

Her colleague was still reeling from the explosion. The blast had knocked him farther away from her position. His attacker kept him at bay, tucking in too close to make the shotgun very useful in the struggle.

"Damn." She couldn't shake the man's grip. She kicked out at him, to no avail. His grasp tightened as the tendrils covered her upper body. With only seconds to act, Morgan kicked her feet back. They hit the wall, and she pushed with everything she had. A scream erupted, exertion and frustration all in one. The tendrils snapped from the sudden shift, and her weight brought her down on top of her attacker. Both crashed to the ground, but Morgan immediately bolted for her freedom.

Each step away from him weakened the strength of his limbs. She spread her arms out, forcing the tendrils to break apart until she was clear. Morgan ran with a fury for Kanigher's position. They needed each other to make any sort of move against the creatures.

"Kanigher, move!"

Kanigher dove out of the way. It wasn't the only reason for her call. When the Bellbrook survivor turned to greet her assault, she smiled. Morgan let loose a punch that slammed into the man's cheek. The blow knocked something loose from his hand. The small device skittered along the ground, for the hole in the window. It was a hard drive, by all appearances.

"No," the man groaned.

He leaped for the drive, which cleared a path for Morgan. She gathered up Kanigher, though her hand screamed the moment she put any pressure on it.

"How bad?" Kanigher snatched his shotgun from the ground, and the pair ran for cover. "The hand?"

"I'm trying not to think about it," Morgan lied. Just touching her knuckles filled her eyes with tears.

"Sounded bad," Kanigher said. "Thanks for the assist."

"You're welcome," Morgan replied. "How about finishing the job for me?"

"Gladly." Kanigher turned and raised the weapon. The Bellbrook survivor scrambled to retrieve his prized possession. With the drive finally in hand, he held it before his eyes with pride. The look faded when the man noticed the weapon pointed at him.

Kanigher pulled the trigger. The shell slammed into the man's chest. He burst into flames in seconds. His entire body was encased in a wall of fire, but the impact of the blast knocked him clear of the building. He appeared to float outside before he fell. His scream filled the air, then silenced at the final impact.

"One down." Kanigher pumped the shotgun to remove the spent shell. He quickly replaced it with a fresh one from beneath.

"If only it was one to go," Morgan said. Kanigher's brow furrowed, and she pointed for the stairwell. Six heavily armed men rushed to the scene, their weapons primed and aimed at the pair of DSA agents. "Looks like we have a new problem."

"We're on your side!" Kanigher called. "We—"

Morgan snatched Kanigher's arm and her hand pulsed with pain. Fighting through the agony, she yanked him down the adjacent corridor a second before the shots started.

Bullets flew freely at their position. The armed assailants offered no warning and no consideration.

"Yeah, I don't think they're going to be real helpful," Morgan said.

Kanigher nodded. "Lucky us."

"Maybe we are."

The Bellbrook survivor roared at the pair of DSA agents. His body seemed to grow in stature, ripping through the ill-fitting suit he wore. Bark enveloped skin as the man barreled toward Kanigher and Morgan.

In doing so, however, he crossed the line of fire. Shots from the security forces slammed into the man-turned-tree. Morgan and Kanigher were no longer at the top of the monster's to-do list. He turned to face the shooters.

Bullets slammed into his chest. Reaching before him, he pushed his hands together. A makeshift shield formed from interlaced fingers.

"What the hell?" one agent asked in disbelief.

"Just keep firing!" another shouted. "Take out all the hostiles!"

"We're trying, but look!"

The Bellbrook survivor was upon them. Through the haze of gunfire, he closed the gap between them. He launched at them, a harsh snarl on his lips. Blow for blow, the man cut through their line. He battered at them, blood and screams filling the corridor.

Morgan fought to stand. Kanigher helped her up, his shotgun at his side. Her chest hurt, her entire body begged for relief, yet she struggled toward the corner and the melee down the hall.

"They're being slaughtered," she said. "Kanigher—"

"I know," he replied. "Dammit, Morgan, I know." He lifted the weapon. "Get them clear. I'll finish this."

Morgan ran into the fray. Shots continued to erupt from the scattered and flailing agents. Their panic was telling, their inexperience the reason the DSA tried to handle things on their own. Diving under the random shots, Morgan waded deeper into the fight.

The Bellbrook man slammed another body across the hall. The poor soul broke through the window before falling to his death. It was an absolute bloodbath. Their guns were ineffective; the agents offered little in the way of resistance.

One by one, they fell before the dominating force of the Bellbrook survivor. His hardened skin and elongated reach proved too much for the set, and by the time Morgan arrived to help, it was far too late.

Standing victorious over the bodies of his victims, the vicious killer caught sight of her approach. "Your turn."

She ducked under his initial strike. His arm swept over her in an arc. She tried to get back to her feet when his other arm shot out. Fingers spread wide like a net and pinned her to the wall.

"Do it, Kanigher!" she yelled. The agent staggered closer, shotgun at the ready. "Do it now!"

He didn't hesitate. He fired the Dragon's Breath at the target. So enamored with Morgan as his next victim, the Bellbrook man failed to defend himself from the attack. The shell caught him in the shoulder and his torso erupted in flames.

His body tumbled to the side. The fire spread rapidly, yet Morgan remained trapped. Heat rushed for her, and the death scream of this strange and unique man boomed in her ear.

"Morgan, you need to move."

"I… know…" she said through clenched teeth. She dropped to the ground to roll under the tendrils of the man's hand. Fire surrounded her. There was no escape.

Morgan ripped off her vest. Wrapping her hands in the fabric, she shoved the man away. The vest protected her hands to some small degree, but she still felt her skin blister and burn. She cried out in pain. With everything she had left, Morgan pushed against the burning bark of his skin.

The hybrid creature fell through the open window. His tendrils snatched the ledge in a last-ditch attempt to save his life. Desperate, they snaked around Morgan's ankle. The man pulled, and she tumbled off the edge.

"No!" Kanigher cried. He dove for the shattered window and grabbed Morgan by the wrist. His free hand snatched the frame. For a moment, he joined them in the open air. Before the fall started, Kanigher's fingers dug around the metal frame of the window and he pulled himself back to the edge. "Let her go!"

"You heard him," Morgan said. She kicked at the tendrils in anger and rising panic. The fingers snapped and broke away with each blow. "Let me go!"

The final tendril cracked, the sound echoing in the air. Limbs flailed in a desperate panic as fire consumed the rest of the hybrid. Morgan watched him fall, possibly the last survivor of the tragedy that occurred in Bellbrook. They had been forever changed, in ways no one would ever believe, and now they were gone, just like the rest.

She wondered how many mysteries might have been solved by studying them. How many diseases could have been cured with their radical treatment? Every positive outcome was lost now.

"You okay?" Kanigher helped her back into the building. He kept her upright when all her body wanted to do was surrender.

"No, but I will be," Morgan said. She looked around at the fallen. Six more had been added to the body count in the last few minutes. An entire building suffered from the devastating attack. Too many lost their lives, thanks to Thirteen and the Witness. "More than I can say for them. Any of them."

# CHAPTER TWENTY-FOUR

Ben couldn't breathe. The fan sucked the air from the chamber with such rapid efficiency, he nearly collapsed. He crouched low to the ground to grab as much air as possible.

Time slipped away quickly. The room had been designed for instant decompression. It was used in case of a fire, or a chemical spill, not at the whim of a madman with delusions of a mass holocaust.

Ben crawled for the wall. There were too many obstructions to see beyond the glass. Tables were upended; the shattering of beakers caused a fog to settle in the main lab. He tried to beat on the glass. It was a useless ploy. Thick enough to withstand an explosion, the sound of his pounding on the glass barely registered as a whisper to the outside world.

In the end, he found himself alone.

It was the only way it could end. Stopping Thirteen from procuring a viral agent was the mission, one vital to the safety of every living soul on the planet. Ben's death paled in comparison.

It was a price Ben had always been willing to pay. The cause was just and the reasoning sound, yet when he repeated the thought tears swelled in his eyes. There were still so many battles to fight and wars to wage. Emily remained lost. The Trust continued to control the world from behind the scenes, changing the shape of the future daily through shell companies and politicians.

Ben had barely made a dent in their ambitions. By the same token, he had barely made a dent in his own. Had this truly been the life he'd wanted? Had he made any difference at all?

He closed his eyes. He imagined a plaque with his name, the

first set to adorn the Bunker's wall. A memorial service would be followed by tears, but quickly replaced by laughter. Or would there be nothing thanks to Metcalf's actions? Would his death be the finishing blow on this latest iteration of the DSA? And then where would they be — his friends and de facto family?

Morgan would be fine. She knew the risks and would continue the fight alone if necessary. Nothing would ever stand in her way, and he hoped he made that clear to her during their short time together. The very thought of her made him smile. Morgan had become more than a partner, more than a friend. She was his lifeline. He should have told her that — told her so many things — and now couldn't.

*Dammit*, he cursed. Ben fought for an ounce of air and found none. His lungs strained for oxygen. He quietly begged for another second of life, another chance to take a stand.

The world blurred before him. The sound of the fan above was lost to his heart pounding in his ears. Ben closed his eyes to the world. As the seconds passed, his heartbeat slowed. Silence accompanied the deepening black. The tremendous weight he'd carried for so long fell away.

In the dark, a rhythmic thrumming surrounded him. It picked up speed and became louder. Ben squinted through the dark to see a burst of light rushing toward him.

The barrier gave way before him. Ben's head slammed against the ground as the glass lifted. Air filled his lungs. It hurt to breathe, and he clung tight to his chest. Ben looked through the blurry world for a sign of life.

He found Metcalf by his side. "Breathe, Ben. Take it nice and slow."

Coughs racked his body. He struggled to sit up. The weight returned, and his body felt the effects. Metcalf's hands met his back to steady his weary frame.

"Metcalf…" he said between coughs. She grimaced at his refusal to relax. Ben hoped for more of a reprieve from her disapproval. He had almost died, after all. "Thirteen —"

"He's gone."

"What?" Surprise filled his eyes. "Why?"

"I had to make a choice," she replied with a warm smile. It was unnatural, but made her look younger than Ben had ever seen her. "Right now? At this moment? You were the right call."

"But the virus?"

Metcalf grabbed the vial behind her and held it before him. "It's safe."

"He left it?" Ben asked. "That doesn't make..." Another wave of coughs stopped him.

"Any sense at all?" Metcalf finished. "I know. I've been asking myself the same thing since he walked away."

"You should have stopped him."

Metcalf patted his back. "So much for gratitude."

"I..." He quieted. She was right, of course. Thirteen might have walked away from the building unscathed, but he hadn't been able to steal any deadly toxins from the restricted level.

Ben let Metcalf's actions hang between them for a long moment. Maybe he had been wrong about her. Maybe a spark of decency was tucked deep inside her, a ray of light capable of holding back the darkness of their task—or her baser instincts.

Metcalf stood, a hand reaching for his own. "Now, if you're up for it?"

He nodded, then took the offer. She helped him to his feet. The second her grip slackened, the floor rose to greet him once more. Metcalf caught him and held tight this time.

"You going to be okay?"

"Yeah," he groaned. "One sec."

She lifted his arm over her shoulder. "Come on. We have to get out of here before—"

The elevator chimed. Masked agents flooded the lab, guns pointed at the shocked pair.

"Uh, Metcalf?" Ben said.

"Hands in the air!" the lead agent shouted. "Don't move!"

# CHAPTER TWENTY-FIVE

"We're federal agents!" Metcalf yelled over the bustling movement of the security forces. Ben kept his hands in the air, afraid to flinch for fear of one of the armed men taking the act the wrong way and finishing the job started by Thirteen earlier. Metcalf's admission did little to endear them to their captors, who secured their hands behind their backs. "I said—"

"Don't care, lady," one replied. "We have hundreds dead, and you're standing in the middle of it."

"Wow," Ben said. "That is some terrible optics."

"Ben…"

"No really," he continued. "We save the day—well, you do—and because we managed to survive, we're guilty of the crime? You sure you're not a detective, pal?"

"Stow it," the man said. He twisted Ben's wrist hard, then shoved him forward. "You can explain yourself outside with the rest of your crew."

"Crew?" Ben laughed. Pain at this point seemed irrelevant, and he pushed past it. "What is this, an *Ocean's Eleven* film?"

Metcalf rolled her eyes.

"You know damn well I'm Clooney in this equation, Metcalf."

"I definitely made the wrong choice," she muttered, as they entered the stairwell and made the climb up to the lobby. "Definitely."

"That's not even funny," Ben shot back.

"That makes two of us, then."

The agents pushed harder, forcing them to climb faster. Spotlights greeted them in the lot. Armed officers took aim, yet relaxed when security led the cuffed pair to the nearest squad car. The agent slammed Ben against the side of the vehicle.

"Don't move."

Ben glared at the man. "Wouldn't dream of it."

"Someone want to take these cuffs off?" Metcalf asked. "We're federal agents."

No one responded. The security team stepped away to clear a path for a second group returning from the building. Morgan's eyes lit up when she caught sight of Ben.

"Ben!" She stopped short, noticing the bruising on his face and the burst blood vessels in his eyes. "What happened? Are you all right?"

"I'll be fine."

Morgan, though, appeared to have been put through a wood chipper. Her hands were blistered, and her skin was covered in scrapes and bruises. The injury to her side from the airport clearly caused her some issues still, as she leaned awkwardly with each staggered step.

Morgan spun toward Metcalf with thin eyes. "What did you do?"

Ben cut between them. "Let it go, Morgan." She backed down from her fighting stance. "You look ready to collapse. What happened?"

Kanigher settled along the side of the squad car. "We met some playmates, had some fun."

"I'll be okay," Morgan said in a soft voice. "Just need to rest."

"Thirteen?" Kanigher asked. Metcalf wouldn't meet the question, her eyes low to the ground.

Ben shook his head. "Escaped."

Kanigher ran his fingers across his eyes. "Not our best day."

"Gee, Kanigher, ya think?" Ben commented.

"Shut up, Riley."

The armed contingent continued to circle them. Guards raced to and from the building but offered little in the way of answers. No one had any, not from the top brass to the agents of the DSA caught right in the middle of it. Thirteen was gone, the Bellbrook Batch dead, with no clear reason behind any of the tragedy that befell the CDC office.

A suited man with fiery red cheeks stepped through the cordon. He flashed his badge to everyone in the area, and the path cleared before him with each interaction.

"I want to know what the hell happened here!" he shouted. Noticing the DSA agents in custody, he immediately clambered over. The badge was out for all to see, HOMELAND SECURITY in bold letters—the name CULLEN listed below. "You hear me? Who the hell are you people, and what in the holy hell have you done here?"

Metcalf cleared her throat. She pushed through the throng of people for the agent. "If you'll allow me to get to my badge, we can have this cleared up—"

"Actually," a voice called from behind the group. The Witness stepped forward. "I believe I can assist with those pesky questions, Agent."

The suited man grumbled. Thin eyes pierced each of them before he stepped away with the Witness. Their words were hushed, but Ben noticed the Witness pass along his badge. Surprise filled Cullen's face.

"How did you know that?" Ben heard the man ask the Witness.

Ben shook his head in disbelief. Even after everything, the Witness still held all the cards. Somehow, he knew Cullen, or at least something about the man, meaning he knew Cullen would be in attendance. Ben flashed back to the image of the man named Joshua Falk and wondered if any of that young, innocent agent remained in the Witness—or if everyone was just a pawn in his game.

A pat on the back ended their little conversation. Cullen moved to coordinate with security on the safety of the building. Local law enforcement joined them. The Witness, however, returned to the team. He carried a small key for their handcuffs and released them.

Ben caught the man's smirk. "Don't look so smug."

"A simple thank you wouldn't be out of line, Agent Riley."

"Would a punch to the face?" Ben asked with a clenched fist. "That's where I'm leaning."

"Enough, Ben," Metcalf said.

"Not even close," Ben snapped. "You said it yourself. Thirteen had the run of the place before we arrived. He walked away with nothing. Does that make any sense to you?"

Morgan jumped between them. "And what about the other

two from Bellbrook? Why were they on the nineteenth floor? One was carrying some kind of hard drive."

"For what?" Kanigher asked.

Ben rubbed his chin. "What was all this for if it wasn't for the virus?"

The Witness stayed quiet. There was no coaxing the answer from him. But for a second, Ben was sure he saw signs of recognition on the man's face. There was an awareness, even behind the blank lenses of his glasses, that some answers were missing from today's events.

"Listen..." Metcalf wrangled the group with a wave. She pulled at them, drawing them close and away from the Witness. Sharp blue eyes met them all. For all the betrayal of the last day, there was still confidence in her stance and hope in her smile. What the rest felt, Ben couldn't say. They struggled to stay awake, the effects of the day finally hitting them as the cool air sought to soothe their wounded bodies. "Things didn't go our way. We have more questions than answers, but we stopped the situation from becoming worse. We will get to the bottom of this."

"We don't have to," Ben said. "He already has, and you know it. So tell us, Glasses, what was Thirteen doing here?"

All turned from their impromptu pep talk. Nothing but the flashing lights of the squad car met their gaze. The Witness was nowhere to be seen.

"Where the hell?" Ben asked in astonishment. They had only taken their eyes off him for a second. "How did he—"

"He's gone, Ben," Metcalf said in a cold, knowing voice. Angry glares shot from the others toward Metcalf. Her distraction had given the Witness all the time he'd needed. But had she planned it that way, or was she as much a victim as the rest?

Ben kicked at the ground in frustration. "So are all our damn answers."

Morgan joined him with a solemn nod. "Again."

# CHAPTER TWENTY-SIX

Zac woke with a start. His head ached from the pressure welling beneath the surface. Surprise filled him when he stood. There was no pain in his limbs, no cuts and bruises from his great fall from the rooftop. He seemed perfectly fine for having tumbled down four stories to the cold concrete.

The room around him came into focus. With pastel colors on the walls, and a floral tile on the ground, recognition set in immediately for Zac. He stood in a kitchen—*his* kitchen. The table sat in the room's center; dishes were stacked neatly along the countertop. Hunched before the sink was someone he never thought he would see again.

"Claire?" he called out.

She didn't flinch at the sound of his voice. Claire continued to work at cleaning up from the meal. His son, Alex, read quietly in the corner.

"Alex!" Zac ran to his son. The boy made no motion, made no sign he heard his father. He simply stared blankly ahead at the pages of his picture book. "Alex?"

Zac tried to get back to them for so long. Now they were here, yet out of reach. Was he dead? Had the fall killed him, and now he was doomed to haunt the lives of his loved ones for all eternity?

"Don't be absurd," a voice answered for him. April stepped into the room. She appeared alive and well again, as if a bullet hadn't ended her life weeks earlier.

"What is this?" Zac asked. "What the hell is this?"

"A place to talk," April said.

"And the fall?"

April winced. "Not your best move. But you're not dead. You'll just wish you were."

Zac read the growing aggravation on her face. "This wasn't you, was it? *I* pulled *you* here to talk, not the other way around."

She sighed, then took a seat at the table.

"They have me, don't they? The Trust," Zac said. April nodded. Closing his eyes, Zac felt his jaw tighten. "They're looking for you, but found me. I can't let them find out the truth."

"Zac..."

"You have to tell me about the signal," he pressed. His hand slammed against the surface of the table. "You were the one who brought it up, but you still haven't told me the whole story. What are you holding back?"

"Don't push this, Zac," April said. "You—"

Pain rushed through his head. He struggled to stay upright. When he opened his eyes, when the agony ripping across his thoughts subsided, the kitchen vanished. In its place was a highway. A giant road sign by the side of the road offered the location he so desperately sought.

"Bismarck," Zac said with quiet awe. "It's in Bismarck."

Concern filled April's eyes. "There is a cost, Zac. There is always a cost."

"Yet you let me know the location."

"You forced the issue."

"Then tell me the rest," Zac said. "Give it all to me. Tell me what happens if I disrupt the signal."

April faded from view. "No. I'm sorry, Zac. You don't want that answer."

"Tell me!" The force of his cry jolted April and locked her in place. Zac circled her. Fury pulsed through his body as he held the presence within his mind. "I control this place. So tell me!"

April struggled against him. "If you break through, if you force me to give you this knowledge, it will be the end of you— of Zachary Modine. The information will cascade, overwriting your memories. You will become the Wellspring, and will stop at nothing to maintain the signal and the plan ahead."

Zac let the words wash over him. The highway disappeared until only a dim fog in his mindscape remained. Zac fell to his knees, releasing April at the same time.

Getting the knowledge to stop what was happening to him

would end his life, just as surely as doing nothing offered the same conclusion. "What do I do then?"

April hovered over him. "Silence the message. Remove your usefulness from the equation. It is the only way for you to be free."

Zac saw the sadness in her eyes. For as much as this was a chance to rid himself of the Wellspring, there was more to it. "What are you still hiding from me? What—"

The fog lifted. The world crashed down upon Zac, and he woke. His body screamed, the pain of the fall immediate and intense. This time, the world was real.

"No." Zac closed his eyes to pull April back into the conversation. He needed to know what she held from him this time. His cry failed to call her to the forefront of his thoughts for answers. Only silence followed his return to reality.

Zac struggled to stand, but the floor jostled beneath him; he was still in motion. He found himself in a transport wagon of some sort. Handcuffs locked his wrists together. He tried to slip the metal bracelets off unsuccessfully. They merely dug into his skin more. Resigned, Zac lay on the floor and waited to reach his destination.

It didn't take long. The car came to a halt in a darkened warehouse. The door of the transport opened, and a pair of soldiers ripped him from the back.

"Hey!" he cried, trying to resist. His body, however, offered little in the way of a fight. He was lucky to still be breathing after his fall.

"This way," a soldier muttered. They dragged him around stacks of crates until the room widened. Armed men in fatigues stood in position on the landing above. They circled the perimeter, keeping watch on everyone down below. Transports rested in a long line. Crates of goods and weapons filled the rest of the space.

A voice cut through the stomping of boots. "You said this would be the end of it."

Zac's eyes widened when the man behind the voice came into view. "Henry." He tried to rush forward, but the soldiers held him back. "Henry!"

The young man argued with another contingent of soldiers. He glanced over at the sound of his name. Sad eyes greeted Zac, the same look offered by April. Henry turned away from him.

"I did as you asked," Henry said. "I brought him in. Now it's time to fulfill your end of the bargain."

A soldier smirked. "Of course. We're men of our word."

"Henry," Zac said. "Help me."

"Like you helped me?" the young man spat. "I'm sorry, Zac. This isn't what I wanted, but I didn't have a choice."

Zac understood. It was an impossible situation, something he was quickly coming to see in everything of late. "I know."

Henry nodded, appreciative of the muted act of forgiveness. The soldiers escorted him to a small room off the warehouse floor.

"Step through here, and we'll conclude our business," the soldier said, his hand firm against Henry's back.

Zac's brow furrowed. "Where are they taking him?"

"He wanted his freedom," the soldier answered. "They're giving it to him."

A single shot echoed through the room.

"No!" Zac pushed off the soldiers. Free from their grasp, he moved for the open door. The returning soldiers barred his path, but not before he saw the dead man lying on the floor inside. "No, no, no…"

He had fought to save Henry. Zac had done everything in his power to give him the peace he'd earned in his life. He had utterly failed in that task.

Tears streamed down his cheeks. Zac collapsed on the warehouse floor, surrounded by armed men.

"Why? Why are you doing this?" No one answered. "All that, and you killed him. For what? What do you want from me?"

"A chance to talk," a voice rang out from the upper floor. Zac couldn't make out the figure through his tear-soaked eyes. He tried to swipe them clean as the man started down the steps for his position.

He wore a tan suit jacket over a white Stafford shirt. His shoes clicked along the metal stairs until they came to rest before him. The man exuded nothing but the utmost confidence and power, as he always had.

David Hollis wore the same self-assured grin he always did.

He crouched before Zac, lifting the broken man's eyes to meet his.

"I think a chat is long overdue, don't you, Zac?" Hollis said. "I want to know everything you're hiding about the Wellspring. And you're going to tell me, or you're going to share Mr. Reed's fate."

# CHAPTER TWENTY-SEVEN

The Witness had little time. He felt the ticking clock the moment he entered the lumber mill north of Millington. This would be the first place the DSA visited once they departed Colorado in the wake of the CDC tragedy.

The attack had only occurred thanks to him. Bellbrook might have been a calculated risk, a necessary one at that, but to see the dead littering the grounds of the CDC made the Witness sick inside. His very presence was meant to help the past in order to save the future. In his arrogance, he'd left himself open to abuse and theft by the man known as Thirteen.

The Witness stalked through the mill. He passed the processing floor for the open space in the back. The three trunks remained in full view. Cracked and torn shells, the Witness eyed each chrysalis with mounting sadness. All his hard work had unraveled.

The Bellbrook Batch had been a critical component in his fight against what came next—against the dark future he'd been forced to view firsthand. He had come back to make a difference, and change humanity's fate for the better.

"Have I simply made things worse?" he asked in the darkness of the mill. Lights were unnecessary. His eyes beheld nothing but what was fed to him through the lenses he wore. Somehow even the Adler woman had seen that much about him—his clever little secret—and what had been his response? He hadn't known her name. The files fed through his display had offered him no clarity on her for some reason.

It was a hole in his plan. So was Thirteen.

Clevinger's science made the signal virus possible, it made

the change a significant enough deterrent to raise against the Trust. Yet again, the Witness had failed to see the truth behind the madman's vision. There had been more than one Clevinger, and this one sought nothing but death and destruction.

The Witness should have known. He should have had some inkling. The plan had been laid out for him, and he took to it willingly. Every instinct screamed for him to do the job without question—to save everyone.

Still, he had not done enough. He kept secrets from the only allies left to him. Wesley had warned him to open up to the DSA. He'd begged for the Witness to trust in someone other than himself for once.

He couldn't. Metcalf had been right. The Witness had held back and continued to do so. In the aftermath, there had been a moment where he'd wanted to share the truth—and explain the damning consequences of Thirteen's theft that went beyond a simple raid on the CDC.

Part of his silence had come from the unknown. He'd been in the dark about Thirteen—a blind spot that required rectifying to continue the mission. The other part, the truer part that made him cringe inside, had been fear. It was fear that in his arrogance, the Witness may well have destroyed any chance of saving the world.

He left the three trunks behind. His steps were muted, but hurried. He fled deeper into the plant. When he exited the back room of the main building, a wide path opened for him. He kicked at the ground, moving through shadows around rows of equipment.

A second structure came into view. It was a storage facility used for overflow, and he had used it in the same manner. Quiet curses followed his movements. The DSA deserved to know the truth behind the situation—the dire circumstances behind the Witness' call for help—yet he'd done everything possible to obscure the facts.

The Witness opened the door to the storage facility. Dozens of open tree trunks lay before him. His shame took hold, and the depths of Thirteen's theft came to light.

He had hoped to change the world for the better. Bellbrook had merely been a stepping stone on a long journey. His arrogance, however, had handed a powerful enemy a tool the Witness could never overcome.

"This is all my fault."

Thirteen now had control over his experiment. Dozens of sleeper agents now worked under his guidance. They learned and grew under Thirteen's ministrations instead of his own. For what purpose, thanks to his fading intel, the Witness held no clue.

And it scared the hell out of him.

# CHAPTER TWENTY-EIGHT

Wilson Dupree opened the front door of his Queens, New York home to the sound of a car backfiring and honking horns. Traffic snarled on the Long Island Expressway, with angry commuters screaming to get to their destination—the same way every morning started.

None of it bothered Wilson. Pure contentment filled his face, and he took a deep breath of the late spring air. It smelled of freshly cut grass after a passing rain shower. The sun crested over the neighborhood; milder days arrived in the brief period before the summer heat took over.

The morning paper sat at the edge of the porch. Wilson held tight to his bathrobe and crouched to snatch the still-wet plastic bag protecting the day's news. When he stood back up, he noticed his neighbor out for her daily jog.

Trish Johnson made a point to pass his place every morning. She wore tight leggings and a tank top that hung much too low for the church-going members of the community. Her dog, Max, raced ahead of her, panting with each hop.

"Looking good, Trish," Wilson called.

She grinned devilishly. Her eyes washed over his chest, clearly visible through the loose bathrobe. Trish stopped her jog, stretching her legs slowly to give him a show. Max yipped at her heels and ran around her in circles.

"Not so bad yourself, Wilson," she said. "See you at the gym later?"

"I'll be there." He pointed to the restless mutt, who continued to bark about the pause in their daily ritual. "Better keep moving."

Her hands fell on her hips, and she leaned to give him a full view of her chest. Trish took in a long breath, feigning another stretch, then released and found her way out of the maze left by her pup.

"He's worse than my ex," she said with a laugh. "So impatient."

"A man on a mission," Wilson replied. "I get that."

Trish notched her sunglasses down from her eyes, an eyebrow cocked with curiosity. "What's your big mission?"

He read the look very well. "This morning? The paper and some eggs." Her disappointment was plain to see. Wilson threw her a wave and grabbed for the door. "I'll catch you later, Trish."

The door closed behind him. The sound of Max barking his way up the block fell away, as did the traffic still snaked around the corner from the early morning rush. Images of Trish carried him through the domicile, his smile intact and growing with each delicious thought.

He passed through the living room without a glance. Two months in, he still failed to find a decent couch for the place, let alone a television. Window dressings were the extent of the decoration, and that was only to keep his neighbors from seeing the emptiness within.

The kitchen was fully stocked, however. He spent most of his time there anyway when he was home. Wilson placed the paper next to the stove, then retrieved a skillet. The burner lit with the flick of a switch. Grabbing an egg from the fridge, Wilson cracked it on the side of the skillet and listened to the sizzle fill the room.

Wilson watched the egg fry. Trish faded to the background, only to be replaced by images of another woman. Her name escaped him. Two children stood before her—his children. They always enjoyed his breakfasts, which were few and far between. There was always work and then, when the divorce happened, Wilson stopped trying altogether.

Still, he recalled the laughter of those mornings. His son used to run around blasting the world in the name of galactic justice, and his daughter bounded from chair to chair with a magic lasso of truth.

They were visions and memories from a former life—one he didn't remember losing, yet could no longer place as his own.

Queens was a far cry from his previous home. It was the opposite of the quiet town of Bellbrook.

He flipped the egg, and the sizzling grew from the act. Two pieces of toast slipped into the toaster, a buzz added to the symphony. Wilson scanned the newspaper.

An incident at the CDC made the front page. Some office in Colorado had been the victim of a terrorist attack. Wilson scanned further through the paper, letting the incident pass. It wasn't important, not to him… not at the moment.

A burning smell wafted in the air. Wilson peered back to the stove and his waiting egg. The skillet was no longer on the burner, resting to the side. His hand, however, sat on the open flame.

Wilson raised it slowly and held the appendage before him. Flesh dripped from his fingertips. He studied the charred hand as if it were a lab specimen. Globs of flesh fell over the stove and splattered beside the skillet.

The toast popped. Wilson grabbed the slices and tossed them on a plate. The egg joined them. Wilson carried the plate with his other hand but kept his curious eye on the burned husk that spread from his wrist. Tendons reconnected, and skin grew back. His fingers rebuilt and danced before his vision.

Bellbrook had changed him. But it was only the beginning.

Wilson settled down at the table for his meal. The plate knocked aside his employee badge, and it clattered to the floor. He bent over to retrieve it, his face decorating the ID. His name ran in thin letters beneath the word SECURITY. An image of the Empire State Building made up the entire background.

No, Bellbrook was behind him. The incident in Colorado had nothing to do with him, either. His work was still ahead, and there was much to do to prepare for his master's arrival.

# CHAPTER TWENTY-NINE

Days of rest afforded Morgan nothing but time to think. As her body slowly healed, a process that would require a longer duration than possible in her line of work, Morgan thought through the events of the last few weeks.

So many secrets had been held back by the members of the DSA. Metcalf remained at the heart of them all, but Ben also carried some of the blame this time around. Trust was essential for the DSA to operate. Divided, everything fell and with it any chance to make the world safer from the likes of the Witness, Thirteen, and who knew how many others still at large.

Thinking about the sabotaging of another led Morgan back to Simon Holbrook. Her insistence on running tests on Ben's blood—as well as keeping it hidden from the public eye—had cost the man his job. She never considered the possibility, never thought of the price he might pay with his discretion. He had been an innocent, and she'd rolled over him without care or concern. It was the same way Metcalf treated the members of the DSA.

Morgan couldn't let that stand. Her behavior was well within her power to change, and it started with Simon.

Morgan stood outside the door to the man's apartment. She didn't bother to tell anyone else where she was headed. Ben had questioned her. Of course, Ben's entire persona thrived on the ability to hold a conversation even without an interested second party. She'd been kind enough not to start a fight over her departure and had promised a swift return. Plenty of other matters needed discussing after her side trip.

Even after convincing herself to make the drive, Morgan

found herself hesitant to act. The cruelty of destroying the man's life without so much as a thank you was enough to bring her hand to the door to knock.

An answer came quickly, though the voice was strained. "Yeah?" Simon called through the door. "Who is it?"

She let out a deep breath. "Agent Dunleavy."

"Oh, hell."

Morgan earned that reaction. She should have taken the samples and run the tests on Ben herself. Fear had made her reach out to a neutral party. Fear of the results, and fear that she might miss something an expert in the field wouldn't ignore. Those were simply justifications, however, for her actions.

"Look," she said. A sigh escaped her, and her head rested on the wood of the door frame. "I know I'm the last person you want to see, but I just want to talk. Two minutes is all I need, and then I'm gone."

In the silence from behind the door, Morgan heard televisions in the neighboring units. Shouts rose from the end of the hall. There was no privacy here, no true living to be had in such squalid conditions.

The lock clicked. The door released from the frame. Simon stood in the shadows, deep bags under his eyes. "Haven't you caused enough problems for me?"

He wore a stained shirt and sweatpants. She nearly fell back from the smell wafting from the apartment. The place probably hadn't had the windows open in years.

She tried to push past that impression and nodded toward the living room behind Simon. "Talk with me, and maybe I can help solve one or two."

He grumbled under his breath, his hand tight to the door. A step back opened the way for her. "Fine. Two minutes."

Minimal furniture filled the room: a couch and television were pretty much it. The lack of clutter, however, didn't stop the cobwebs from making their presence known in every corner of the living space. The kitchen was off the back of the room. Dishes piled up in the sink, and day-old pizza sat on the table.

Simon circled the room, curious glances thrown in her direction as he collected the pizza and jammed it in the fridge. When he returned to the living room, he stopped short of the couch and leaned along the back.

"What happened to you?"

Morgan shook her head, confused. "What do you mean?"

"You have a slight limp," Simon said. "You're trying not to hold your side, but your hand moves to it with each breath. That doesn't even take into account your other hand, which you're trying not to use at all. You've been in quite the fight, I'd say."

"You would be right."

Simon pushed from the couch. He ran his hand through the uneven tufts of hair on his head. "All right, wait here. Let me see what I can do to help."

"I don't—"

"Just give me a minute." Simon started for the hall off the kitchen. "Don't touch anything."

Morgan glanced around the room. She rolled her eyes and muttered under her breath, "You couldn't pay me to touch anything in this place."

Something, though, caught her eye as she waited for Simon to return. An open photo album sat on the arm of the couch. The pages displayed pictures of many young boys. A few appeared identical, but most bore slight differences in appearance and posture. Their attitudes also appeared unique—some with pure smiles and others with more sarcastic wit behind their eyes. All stared brightly ahead, except for one young man in the middle of the second page. He had his back turned to the camera, his face completely hidden from view.

Simon stepped into the room. Bandages and ointment bottles filled his hands. At the sight of her over the arm of his couch, his movements quickened, and he closed the distance. He dropped the supplies on the cushion, then reached to gather up the album.

"Cute kids," Morgan said. "Big family?"

"Cousins," Simon replied hurriedly. He closed the album and tucked it under the television. "And nephews. Yes. It's a big family. Or it used to be, anyway."

"I didn't see too much of a resemblance."

Simon pointed to a scar under his ear. "I've had work done. There was an accident."

"I see," Morgan said, ashamed at pressing the issue.

"Most don't," Simon said. He retrieved the bandages. "Now let me take a look."

He set to work on her. He removed her bandage carefully, though it still caused her immense discomfort. Rubbing on some ointment, he lightly spread the balm around the bruise that occupied much of her side. Then he wrapped the wound.

Morgan winced. Agony gripped her, and she sucked in quick breaths to deter from crying out. She looked back at the closed photo album. "You said you used to have a big family. They don't come around anymore?"

"We had a falling out," Simon answered, his focus on dressing her wound.

"I had the same thing happen with my brother," Morgan said. "I'm still trying to make things right between us."

Simon finished. He settled along the couch, dropping the gauze at his side. "What is this, Agent? An intervention?"

"No, I—"

"Did you come for a personal history?"

Morgan ran her hand over the bandage. She pulled her shirt back into position. "No," she said in a soft voice. "I came to offer you a second chance."

"That office was my second chance," Simon spat. "I blew it. Same with everything else in my life."

"I don't believe that's true," Morgan said. His diagnosis of the woman at the clinic had impressed her. He had refuted his superior's findings and spoken out about it despite her animosity toward him. All had been done with innate knowledge and evidence to back up his assertion. It hadn't gone unnoticed by Morgan, who thought the DSA could stand to learn a lesson or two from the man.

Morgan bent low at the edge of the couch. "I can't make up for costing you your job, and you have every right to tell me to get out and never come back, but I'm hoping you'll think over my offer."

"What—"

"Come work for me," she said. "With my team."

"The FBI?" Simon asked in a surprised tone.

Morgan's hand flew to her brow. "No. We're not..." She paused, a laugh caught between her lips. How the hell had Grissom made this sound so easy when he'd recruited her? "That was a cover. I work for the DSA."

"Never heard of it."

"Then we're doing our job well," Morgan said. "We could use a man with your skills, Simon. Your knowledge of pathology and biological systems will help us in our work. It's not... We're not talking about a private practice or a fancy lab, but it's good work."

Simon crept toward the edge of the couch. "I—"

Morgan waved him down as she stood. "You don't have to answer now. I can come back and we can—"

"Yes."

Morgan's eyes widened. "Yes?"

Simon looked around the shabby living room. "What the hell have I got to lose?"

# CHAPTER THIRTY

Ben paced the corridor in the Bunker. Hands clasped tight to the image behind his back as he created a circuit down the domicile wing and back again in an endless loop. Nerves kept him moving. He'd wanted to reach out to her the second they'd arrived back home, especially after they'd found nothing but ashes and rubble at the Witness' lumber mill in Millington following the CDC attack.

Instead, silence had taken over. It didn't come from his side of the conversation, though he completely understood the lack of response. There had been too much mistrust over the mission, and the lack of any answers in the way of Thirteen's strike had left them cold. They carried that isolation all the way back to the Bunker.

Ben had been left to contemplate matters for far too long. Now, with his nerves up and the conversation on repeat in the back of his mind, he simply waited for the opportunity to make things right.

When Morgan finally arrived, Ben nearly slipped and fell. His surprise came not only from her sudden return, but from the exhausted look in her eyes. Her entire body appeared ready to collapse, the wounds from Colorado still dogging her every move.

Ben cut her off in the middle of the corridor. "And where have you been, young lady?"

Morgan worked around him for her door. She opened it and let out a long sigh. "I'm tired, Ben. I can't—"

"Hey," he called, the sarcasm lost behind concern. "Is everything all right? Where were you?"

"I—"

"Is it your side?" The way she leaned against the frame caused her shirt to lift slightly. Ben noticed a fresh set of bandages along her midsection. "Did something—"

"It's nothing, Ben," Morgan said. "I mean, it hurts like hell, but I'm fine. Really."

He cocked an eyebrow in disbelief.

She smirked. "I'll be fine."

Morgan headed into the darkness of her room. The door slowly closed behind her.

Ben bit his lip. Unwilling to let his opportunity slip away, he stepped forward to block the door with his foot. "I found out his name."

The door stopped. Morgan's hand lingered on the knob. Curious eyes met his.

"That's what I was holding back," Ben continued, filling the silence between them. "Not for any reason other than I was still processing what it meant, what it still means, if anything."

Curiosity turned to confusion. The exhaustion returned and Morgan ran her hand through her hair. "Ben, I—"

"He's Joshua Falk, Morgan," Ben said. "The Witness. That's who he is."

"What?" Morgan took a step back, then shot into the corridor. "What do you mean he's... How do you—"

Clutched between Ben's fingers was a single image, the one that had tripped up his every thought since discovering it. He passed it along to Morgan. "It was tucked between the files. I think Wes wanted us to know."

Her eyes grew wider with each second spent on the photo. In it, Wesley Fuller stood beside his partner, Joshua Falk, who wore the signature black fedora and round spectacles of the Witness. The image had been taken in 1972, yet Falk had barely aged.

"This is..." Morgan paused. She lowered the image and all it implied, then fell back against the door frame. "I don't even have the words."

"That's how I felt too," Ben replied. "But it doesn't make up for keeping this from you."

"Ben..."

He waved her down. "Just listen, Morgan."

"Okay."

"I thought it was over for me in Fort Collins. After so many close calls, you'd think I'd be used to it... but all I could think about was your disappointment in me." Ben let out a deep breath. He leaned close, unable to meet her gaze—afraid the words would fail and the silence would take hold again. "You're too important to me, Morgan, to let secrets come between us. So, this is me saying there won't be any."

Her hand grazed his arm. She squeezed lightly. "Ben. That's—"

A throat cleared from behind Ben. Both spun to see Kanigher in the corridor, his hands deep in his pockets. "Sorry to interrupt."

Morgan stepped away from the door frame and from Ben. "That's all right, Kanigher."

"Not really, though," Ben grumbled.

Kanigher winced. "Yeah. I didn't think so." He pointed down the hall. "I could come back."

"Could you?" Ben pressed.

"Riley."

He read Morgan's tone well enough. There was more to say, but there always would be.

Ben sighed. "Fine. What's going on?"

Kanigher nodded. "I've gathered the others as well. It's time we talk about where we go from here."

# CHAPTER THIRTY-ONE

They had been in a holding pattern for days. Each of the members of Metcalf's team needed the time. There were wounds to heal, tempers to calm, and worries to ponder in the silence of the Bunker, away from everyone else.

Metcalf had kept her distance. She'd circled through the Bunker each morning to collect anything she might have needed, then retreated to her quarters. Rest was required, but it had also afforded her team time to move past the rifts that had formed thanks to the Witness' arrival.

With the training room available, Metcalf headed there for a workout. All her frustration and anger over Thirteen and the Bellbrook tragedy was taken out on the robotic dummies that cropped up in increasing numbers daily. Nixon seemed to use all his free time to add to the arena. No doubt he would be in there again to replenish their supply once Metcalf was through.

She had screwed up. Ben had been correct in his assessment. He had given her the chance to come clean, to move in front of her secret with the Witness, but she never bothered. Her lack of trust in the team cracked their precarious foundation. As much as they needed the reprieve from her orders and her directives, they needed a break from her more.

Metcalf wondered how long it would last. She worried their downtime played perfectly into the hands of the Trust: that without the DSA actively investigating at all times, the shadowy organization run by Hollis would make their next move. If the team wasn't prepared, both mentally and physically, the world might pay the price.

Four days in, and the worries won out. Metcalf needed to

move, to act, and the price of her past mistakes be damned. The team would fall in line. They had to for the good of the mission, and that was the only thing that truly mattered in the long run.

Metcalf left her quarters behind. She put away the frustrations taken out on much too realistic robotic dummies and decided to focus on work. When she reached the Operating Theater, Metcalf realized she was not the only one with the idea.

The entire team sat around the conference table. The monitors continued to run silent, but the conversation was lively between them. Adler sipped at her coffee, her tablet before her. Nixon chomped on some trail mix in between typing stints. He added little to the discussion, his mind on another task.

The conversation split between Kanigher, Morgan, and Ben for the most part. Their words came in hushed tones. Anger and aggravation rose to fill the rest of the room. Their talk came to a grinding halt when she reached the top of the stairs.

Metcalf crossed her arms, her cold eyes washing over them all. "I assume this gathering is for my benefit?"

Guilty glances ran from agent to agent. Adler's cheeks flushed with embarrassment. Nixon didn't bother to look up, clearly reading the tension in the room. His computer was definitely the safer bet.

Ben slowly stood from the table to speak. "We've been talking it over."

Morgan nodded. "This doesn't work, Metcalf."

The anger in Morgan's voice jolted everyone to the reality of where they were. Her rage continued to surprise Metcalf. It grew with their every interaction, and nothing Metcalf said calmed the frayed edges of their relationship. The anger hurt Metcalf more than she could say, more than she would say considering her inability to emotionally connect with the people in the room. Morgan had been Metcalf's first true recruit to the Bunker. Everything she'd done had been to save her from Sullivan's coup, from the fall of the original DSA.

Morgan saw none of that in her superior. To her, Metcalf was the root cause of all their suffering. Metcalf could hardly fault her thinking on the subject.

Ben waved Morgan down to her seat. "Morgan, please."

"Let her talk, Ben," Kanigher said. He had obviously made his choice in the matter, something Metcalf never imagined possible given their history.

Ben hesitated, then sat back down. Morgan stood from her chair, leaning against the edge of the table. "You knew about the Witness and kept it from us for months. A known murderer. A terrorist, by any definition. You've worked with him, defended him, and kept his secrets."

"We can't trust you, Susan," Kanigher said. "And you sure as hell don't trust us."

"So, this is what… my intervention?"

"No," Ben replied. His eyes begged for her to listen, for her to understand and make things right. "This is your chance to come clean. About everything."

"No more lies," Kanigher said.

Ben nodded. "You lay it all on the table. The secret history of Susan Metcalf."

Morgan's gaze thinned. "The truth we've deserved from the start."

# CHAPTER THIRTY-TWO

"You're still here?"

Interim Project Leader Franklin North entered the shadowy storage level of the CDC's Fort Collins branch. His enthusiasm grew at the presence of another in the room. Paige Hammond turned at his arrival, the distraction enough to let her note the late hour on her watch. She rubbed at her eyes, then quickly gathered her belongings.

Franklin stopped at her side. "I have to say, Dr. Hammond, it's been an honor having you aboard during this difficult time. I had no idea how much work would be involved when they brought me in to clean up the mess left from the attack. When your name came up in our system as someone who could help get us back on our feet, I never realized how much help that would be."

She didn't bother to answer. A mere smirk and a nod perked up her superior. He sidled closer, his hand falling upon her back.

"I have to say, I had never even heard of your work in the field before finding your record on our server," Franklin said. "How you managed to hide from the world astonishes me."

"It was easy," she replied. "It's all made up."

Franklin backed a step. Confusion shifted to laughter. The strong bellows made up for his awkwardness. "That was a good one."

"It certainly was," Paige said with a grin. She stood from her stool. Her bag rattled at her side, the top open and contents visible within.

"What do you have there?" Franklin leaned over to see several vials taken out of storage. His eyes flared with recognition, especially the contents of the top vial, which read BLAKE in large letters. "What are you doing with those specimens?"

Franklin moved for her terminal. All the records had been erased pertaining to the items in Paige's possession. Every digital backup and physical documentation had been purged. She made sure of that before he entered the room. Her work of the last few weeks had granted her access to the available information. The procurement of the specimens was the last piece of her mission.

"What have you done?"

"I should thank you for the opportunity," Paige said. He tried to reel away from her approach, but she grabbed him by the shirt and held him close. Her fingers slid to his neck. Wrapping tight around his throat, Paige lifted the man from the ground. "But the constant groping, and the nauseating flirting, has really made this a terrible job."

"How…" Franklin gasped. "Who are you?"

"The future." Paige brought him back down and held him before her. She pointed a single finger at his terrified eye. It grew, branching forward, and cut through his iris into his brain.

The movement was so sudden, Franklin didn't have a chance to scream. His body simply seized from the act and collapsed to the ground. A single drop of blood slid along the side of his nose like a stray tear.

Paige grabbed her gear, closing the secure pouch of her bag to hide the vials. She stepped casually over the broken body of the Interim Project Leader and headed for the door.

Security stood down the hall. The man in question, Reggie, smiled at her. With a tip of his cap, he accepted her ID badge.

"He convince you to head home?"

"I hate to upset the boss," Paige said with a laugh. "He said he might be awhile."

"I'm sure," Reggie said. His eyes rolled at the thought of the long night ahead of him. "See you tomorrow?"

Paige said nothing. A wave back to the man was her only response as she started for the exit. There would be no coming back tomorrow, not after they discovered the body in the room. That, however, would not come for some time, long enough for her to clear the building.

Her mission was at an end: the true mission of her master's

visit to the office. Where everyone looked to the explosions and the potential theft of a single contagion as motive enough for the act, her master had planned leagues ahead of any of them. The visit to the restricted level had been nothing more than a feint—a chance to build his shopping list for the real theft.

The trip to the nineteenth floor had been the true purpose behind their assault on the CDC complex. Not to steal information, but to plant it within the system. The data encrypted on the server opened the door for Paige to insert herself into the recovery process. With so many fresh faces brought in to get the office back up to speed, it had been a simple task to infiltrate their operations.

Why settle for one contagion, one threat everyone would prepare for, when you could steal more they had no idea about in the first place?

Paige's wicked smile carried her from the building. No one questioned her. No one attempted to stop her or track her belongings. They knew her by name and believed her to be nothing more than a lab tech cataloging information.

Leaving the parking lot behind, Paige found a car waiting for her at the end of the block. She opened the back door and slipped inside. Tires squealed, and the vehicle was in motion before she was seated properly.

"Success, my dear?" Thirteen asked. He sat across from her, twin flutes of champagne in his hands.

"Of course," Paige answered. She opened her bag. The vials rattled innocently inside.

He passed her a glass and raised his own. "To the future."

She clinked the glass, then took a sip. Laughter filled the back of the car, hidden from the rest of the world. Her master's plans were just beginning. Thirteen had won, and no one would be ready for the nightmare to come.

# ABOUT THE AUTHOR

Lou Paduano is the author of the Greystone series of urban fantasy adventures, which follow Detective Greg Loren and Soriya Greystone as they hunt myths, monsters, and legends in the city of Portents.

He is also the author of the conspiracy thriller series, The DSA, a serialized tale about a clandestine government agency trying to discover the true power behind humanity's future.

Lou lives with his wife and three daughters in Grand Island, NY. You can learn more about his books, including upcoming releases and free content by visiting his website at loupaduano.com.

# THE GREYSTONE SAGA

**AVAILABLE NOW**

Follow the adventures of Soriya Greystone and Detective Greg Loren as they hunt dangerous myths and legends in the city of Portents.

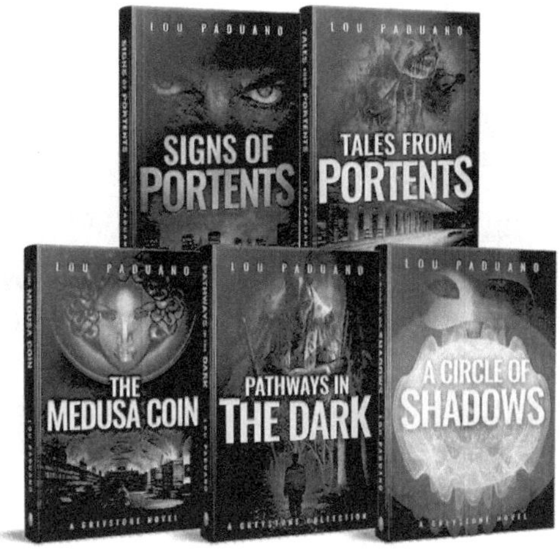

**BOOK ONE - SIGNS OF PORTENTS**
**BOOK TWO - TALES FROM PORTENTS**
**BOOK THREE - THE MEDUSA COIN**
**BOOK FOUR - PATHWAYS IN THE DARK**
**BOOK FIVE - A CIRCLE OF SHADOWS**

# GREYSTONE-IN-TRAINING

## AVAILABLE NOW

For years, Soriya trained to become the Greystone.
Follow the trials that made her the protector
Portents needed to fend off the darkest of threats.

**BOOK ONE - HAMMER AND ANVIL**
**BOOK TWO - THE GIFTS OF KALI**
**BOOK THREE - THE FINAL GAUNTLET**

# THE DSA CONTINUES IN…

Judgment day arrives for the DSA.

Susan Metcalf's connection to the Witness comes to light and threatens everything the team has fought for. Trust breaks. Divisions form among the members, forcing them to choose sides. Before things fall apart completely, the DSA must decide the fate of one of their own.

Not only have Metcalf's secrets come back to haunt the team, a figure from her twisted past arrives to plague to team at their absolute lowest point. Vivian Ness lost everything thanks to Metcalf, and plans to do the same not only to Metcalf, but the rest of the DSA team.

The origin of the DSA stands revealed on the eve of its very destruction in the penultimate chapter of the stunning second season.